The Book of Mistaken Journeys

SUNDIAL HOUSE

The Book of Mistaken Journeys

Clara Obligado

Translated by

Molly Wagschal

SUNDIAL HOUSE

SUNDIAL
HOUSE

Book and cover design: Lisa Hamm

Cover art: Cecilia Mandrile

Copyediting: Vivian Arimany, Miranda Mazariegos, Emily Oliveira,
Daniela Ordóñez Delgado, and Nínive M. Vargas de la Peña

ISBN: 979-8-9903224-3-1

Contents

I live my life in widening rings.
The last ring, in spite of my trying, I doubt—
As it wanders across and over things—
if I shall ever complete.
(. . .)
Am I falcon, or storm,
or song, an immense song?

—Rainer Maria Rilke, *The Book of Hours*
(trans. Susan Ranson)

For Roco, always by my side

Translator's Note

THE TITLE of Clara Obligado's short-story collection, *El libro de los viajes equivocados* (*The Book of Mistaken Journeys*), presents readers with an enigma: How could a "viaje" (journey, trip, voyage) be "equivocado" (mistaken, wrong, erroneous)? Born in Buenos Aires in 1950, Obligado is no stranger to the enigmas of migration. In 1976, following the military coup in Argentina, she went into exile in Spain. Despite the possibility of returning to her home country after the fall of the military junta, she chose to stay in Madrid, where she has now lived for the majority of her life. This prolonged state of "extranjería" (foreignness) that Obligado describes as a condition of permanently living outside of Argentina plays a central role in her work. Indeed, almost all of the characters in *The Book of Mistaken Journeys* have migrated for various reasons—war, state violence, disaster, opportunity, love—and all feel fundamentally out of place. The work is a collection of eleven short stories, set in locations as diverse as Argentina, the Arctic Circle and Albania, and in time periods ranging from the prehistoric era to the 21st century. And yet, as one starts to grasp in an initial reading, all the stories are interrelated. Some appear more clearly linked than others—for instance, those with recurring characters. However, even when individual plots seem disparate in time and place, reading the stories together forms a larger network of subtle linguistic and thematic repetitions.

Each of the stories in the collection is complete on its own, but reading them together creates additional layers of narrative that an isolated reading precludes. *The Book of Mistaken Journey's* hybrid narrative style thus bends genre conventions, as the book falls somewhere between a novel and a collection of short stories. Obligado's insistence on the short-story genre can perhaps be seen as a way of bridging the gap between what Mikhail Bakhtin called the "polyphonic novel" and the rich history of the Latin American short-story, continuing the tradition of celebrated writers such as Gabriel García Márquez, Julio Cortázar, and Jorge Luis Borges, the last of whom Obligado studied with in Argentina. Along with the collection's thematization of migration and its unique form of polyphonic prose, the image of the spiral emerges as a central feature, as if to organize the diverse voices and stories contained in the book. The first story in *The Book of Mistaken Journeys*, titled "Chance," introduces the reader to the practice of what I will call spiral reading; that is, reading with attention to thematic and linguistic repetitions in an effort to trace widening circles in the work and reconstruct textual spirals—small and large.

The story "Chance" opens with two characters, Lyuba and Jan (who will reappear later on), on a beach in what we later discover is Normandy, France. Lyuba discovers a spiraling conch shell in the sand and discards it, but Jan takes an interest in the conch: "Peering into the tiny windows that time has opened in the conch, he recognizes a logarithmic spiral; those ones that spin, widening around an infinitesimal point." Here, Obligado describes the logic of the spiral that organizes the book. It starts from an "infinitesimal point" and expands in widening curves that repeat and evolve (evoking Rainer Maria Rilke's epigraph). Following this logic, if one were to focus only on the smallest curves, she would not see the full spiral; one may not even realize that she is looking at a spiral. Therefore, it is necessary to take a step back and observe these recurring curves from a distance. Only then will the greater spiral be revealed. I propose a reading of *The Book of Mistaken Journeys* that follows the same logic of this logarithmic spiral: if we read each story on its own, we see only the curve that it creates, but once we start connecting the stories to each other, we see that together they form widening curves, and eventually culminate in the textual spiral that Obligado has reproduced as a paratext at the end of the book. The spiral structure that emerges would explain Obligado's insistence, in her "Author's Note," on reading the stories in the order they appear. My hope is that each reader will find connections that she finds curious or meaningful in the work and pursue them through her own practice of spiral reading.

To conclude, I would like to offer a few reflections on my translation of *The Book of Mistaken Journeys*, and on translation as a mode of textual interpretation. Postcolonial theorist Gayatri Spivak famously stated that "translation is the most intimate act of reading." That is, we can think of translation not just as a written transmission of the source text into a different language but also as a closer way to approach the source text as readers. Translation as a form of close reading is particularly useful in the context of *The Book of Mistaken Journeys*, a work that needs to be read multiple times to apprehend the full range of connections between the stories. In the process of translating the collection, I read and reread each story many times, considering it as a full unit and also in relation to the others. Upon each reading, I discovered new details and connections, and I suspect that additional readings would continue to unearth even more curves and spirals. Reading the collection with the intention of translating it also enabled me to identify recurring terms that link the stories. For example, the repetition of the verb "bambolear" (to sway, wobble, lurch) to describe the body of the mammoth being excavated in "Cold," the red balloon released by the little girl in "Black Holes," and Kristina's body atop her unsteady shoes in "Albania" invited me to explore how these stories are connected thematically. Of course, an attentive reader could identify linguistic repetitions without the intention of translating; what I want to argue is that the intimacy between the translator and the source text naturally encourages a closer reading. My goal in translating *The Book of Mistaken Journeys* has been to create a version that flows in English while honoring the unique Spanish prose. Obligado writes in a dense, literary Spanish that is often difficult to recreate in English without altering syntax and punctuation. In my translation, I have attempted to emulate this dense prose while making the necessary syntactic adjustments, sometimes substituting a semicolon or dash for a comma and occasionally breaking up sentences. Above all, I have tried to honor the repeating motives and terms that are so central to the spiral of the work, translating them consistently whenever possible.

Translating *The Book of Mistaken Journeys* would not have been possible without the help of readers, editors, and interlocutors. I would like to thank Michelle Clayton, Mateo Lu Tsai, Steven Wagschal, Lucas Joshi, Katerina Ramos-Jordán, Andrés Emil González, David Parsard, and the members of Denise Kripper's ALTA workshop for reading some form of this translation and offering me generous feedback. Thank you to Sundial House and to Eunice Rodríguez Ferguson for her constant support and enthusiasm for this project. A huge thanks to Juan Casamayor of Páginas de Espuma for facilitating this transatlantic literary connection, and to Clara Obligado for welcoming me into her home in Madrid and answering my endless questions with grace and wisdom. And lastly, thank you to Abel Castaño Bravo and Erica Durante for leaving me a copy of *El libro de los viajes equivocados* in Fall 2023 and starting this journey.

Author's Note

I BEGAN writing this book in the course of writing my last book, where I contemplated the meaning of exile. Years later, I found myself thinking about the implications the diaspora carries in the lives of those who set forth in it. In this moment of crisis, the notion of the journey brought me back to past eras and to certain ideas I thought had already been extinguished. This coming and going, this spiral, is the story behind my stories. All I ask of readers is that they read the stories in the order they appear, as together they conceal a larger text that relies on this path.

The Book of
Mistaken Journeys

Chance

To Jorge Payá, for his good ideas

LYING DOWN on the beach, Lyuba takes off her bikini top, digs her back into the warm sand, and feels a pinch. It's a conch shell shining under the sun; it looks like it's been there for a long time. Without giving it much thought, she brushes the shell aside and closes her eyelids, which diffuse a red glow. Next to her, Jan prepares for a test that will determine his future. He's crazy about Lyuba but doesn't dare tell her; soon it will be time to go home, so he needs to speak now or let it go already. He picks up the shell and studies it. Peering into the tiny windows that time has opened in the conch, he recognizes a logarithmic spiral; one of those that spin, widening around an infinitesimal point. He decides to place it on Lyuba's navel: if the shell stays balanced for more than two minutes, he'll ask her to marry him. If it falls off, he'll go back to his home country and distance himself from her, just like those infinite circles distance themselves from the shell's center. As he's reaching out his hand, he sees that Lyuba has a strange navel that protrudes outwards, making it impossible to sustain an object. In the sky, a peregrine falcon draws ever-widening curves, each one more open than the last.

Forty years before this scene, a young woman prowls along the brush. Night has fallen, and in this rainy June, the vegetation feels even denser. She carries an apple in her pocket; it's all she has to eat. Perhaps she will find something if she combs around at night—the Germans ought to be asleep at their watch posts. Besides, hunger is stronger than fear, and she has good legs for running. She looks up at the sky and sees a breathtaking shower of parachutes floating down, like beautiful, expectant comets. She watches them until, in the distance, gunfire rings out. The young woman runs and hides, tripping and falling face-first onto a soldier who seems to be asleep but has his eyes open, almost transparent, gazing at the sky as if posing a question. He's not German; the Germans don't wear that uniform. Careful not to stain herself with the rampant blood, she looks through his pockets, finds a medallion, some foreign coins, an iridescent conch shell, and a photograph. She pockets the money and throws the shell towards the shore. Suddenly, two enormous hands grip her neck. A German soldier rips the money away from her, furiously repeating the word "dollar." Walking away with her hands behind her head, she realizes that if only she had tossed the money instead of the shell, she could have saved her life.

Nearly two centuries earlier, a girl strolls along that same beach. She thinks about her father, who cares more about money than anything else, and her mother, who is now blatantly cheating on him. Between her mother's raging freedom and her father's greed, the girl prefers her mother. She hates this wasteland, this wretched village where no one dreams of anything. Winter has sunk its hooks into the gray sea. The girl jumps, sheltering her petticoats from the waves' lace. Her damp boots trace a line of salt in the sand. She picks up a conch shell to play with on her way home. In the living room, sitting by the fire, her mother seems to float above the afternoon's sorrow. She's flaunting a new dress, her hair swirling, her cheeks ablaze. The girl decides to surprise her with a gift and puts the shell in her purse, where her hand collides with a piece of paper. She holds the paper in her fist and waits, beaming, for her mother to come give her a kiss. But the mother is tired of this girl. She finds the shell, holds it between two fingers, muttering, who put this garbage here, shoves her daughter and shirks away. That night under the covers, the girl reads the promissory note that her mother signed to a moneylender. She walks on her tiptoes and leaves the note unfolded on her father's table. In the morning, she hears the shouting and smiles to herself, snug beneath the blankets.

Centuries back, also in Normandy, a crowd advances. The plague has broken out, and prophets are selling the people salvation, or—when that fails—threatening them with the stake. Desperate mothers throw their newborns into the sea, as if rocking back and forth in the waves were a gentler torment than life itself. Warrior maidens promise to lead the people to safety, and, though skeptical, they follow, ultimately fueled by faith. Some march towards an unknown fate; others fall back with the carts carrying the sleeping dead. When exhaustion overtakes them, they are left on the side of the road, with no time to close their eyes. Everyone trembles, except for a girl who smiles and trots behind the crowd. She doesn't have a family, at least not one that she remembers; all she has are the clothes on her back and a conch shell she picked up on the beach. She does somersaults to earn a few coins and receives them larded with harsh words, which don't bother her because she is deaf. The blows on the other hand, the blows do hurt her; that's how she lost her hearing, and since then she has sworn to get revenge. Next time they touch me—she tells herself—next time. And one day the time comes, when a soldier is shoving a young woman towards the stake. The girl, playing behind him, reaches out her hand, and the soldier, irked by the crowd's silence and the condemned woman's sobbing, strikes the girl, ripping off the shell that hangs from her neck. The girl spits out a tooth. At night, she picks a hot coal from the sleeping embers and approaches the hay cart where the soldier lies snoring. A while later, the village is ablaze and the soldier howls, his mane in flames.

It's far too cold on this dusk from two hundred thousand years ago. In the distance, the pack crowds around the fire. It's starving, devouring itself. There is nothing to hunt or fish this winter; the blades of grass cannot break through the ice. The darkened forest appears dead, and the snow falling amid the giant trees instantly erases any trace of prey. One female has fallen behind; she can no longer keep up with the group, and there's no time to get to the cave, where she could rest on the furs. She's alone on the beach, weighed down by her belly. She has felt afraid for a while now. Afraid and out of time. How will she survive out there on the ice? What will she do all alone until it gets warm? The sea is an infinite field of solid ice. The hard blows coming from her belly force her into a squat. She has never given birth, and her mouth fills with saliva, knowing that the jumbled mass about to emerge could be her salvation. She also knows it will not be easy. Blood, so much blood rushes between her legs, the blood always comes first. Thick, red blood—hot, nourishing. She bellows out, clutching her knees, pushing and roaring, the labor is breaking her. Just when she is nearing exhaustion, when she can't take it anymore, something finally drops. The female sniffs the sticky mess, stirring and prodding it with her muzzle. She's about to lick up the blood, opening her jaws over the appetizing body. It's so easy to pounce on this defenseless, warm meal that is starting to wail; her throat floods with saliva and hunger. Suddenly, she spots a glimmer in the snow covering the beach. It's a shining conch shell, and for a second it distracts from her insatiable hunger. The moon has risen, lighting the object in an iridescent glow. The female, exhausted, feels that in some part of her body an unfamiliar emotion is stirring. Everything is shining under the pallid light; in this strange silence the sky is a starry rapture. She closes her jaws, clenches her teeth and contains herself. Taking the flint she carries on her waist, she pierces the shell's surface, traces a sign, and hangs the talisman around her daughter's neck.

When the world was a boundless blue ocean, when all forms of life were aquatic and the only things on land were barren rocks, the first gastropods emerged, dragging themselves to shore. This was more than five hundred million years ago. Perhaps the patient marine salts allowed their skin to amass those beautiful layers, maybe it was meticulous chance that sculpted them, inscribing their shells with a growing spiral. Beautiful but defenseless, they skipped around the untamed waves, whistled in the sea foam, floated. And so, propelled by the sea, a conch shell reached the shore. There were hardly any clouds, the emerging lands floated south and Europe was barely an island on whose beach the mollusk landed, began to writhe, replicated itself, then widened its rings until they became whirlpools, hurricanes, galaxies.

The Two Sisters

For Martín Kohan

ON THE day he left Poland forever, Jan Siedlecki rose when it was barely morning and heard his mother making breakfast as he dressed. He ate his bread in silence. Later, with his cheek resting on her hair as kissed her goodbye, he knew the separation to come would be as long and hard as death, given that she did not know how to write.

Already on his way, he turned and glimpsed the closed shutters on his bedroom window. His mother would go in there to clean, drying her tears on her apron. She would let the first glimmer of light peer in and then, maybe for years, everything would stay the same: the bed with its patchwork quilt, the wardrobe and its jingling hangers, the table where Jan had abandoned his books and pen forever, unable to carry anything else.

The steep road led him towards the bakery, where his older brother was baking rye bread for the whole village. Since their father's death, he had taken over the shop, which barely earned enough for them to eat. Only on the eve of Yom Kippur, when the villagers clamored for kugel baked following the recipe of their ancestors, did the family's coffers briefly grow and then dwindle again, once the festivities had ended. The bread's aroma bade Jan an olfactory farewell. He didn't enter to say goodbye to his brother; instead, he patted the head of his puppy, who followed behind in leaps.

He had barely slept the night before. It was the first time he had held his fiancée in his arms; they met behind the bakery, taking advantage of the silent village to embrace each other. He promised to send for her then, and she told him that she would be his wife. It was also then that he swore he would never kiss another woman. Their embraces went so far that if Jan's brother had not started shuffling around the bakery, the young woman's honor might have been in peril. Jan had caressed Anastazja's breasts for the first time, and now he breathed in his hands until he could smell that warm fragrance blended with the scents of dawn, firewood and bread.

The beautiful Anastazja had risen at dawn to see him go. Peering out the window, her disheveled and tearful face lit by an oil lamp, she blew a kiss into the air and tossed him her portrait wrapped in a handkerchief. Then, for a brief moment, another face appeared: her older sister, holding her in a seeming embrace. Ruth was much plumper than

Anastazja, her dark hair gathered into a braid and a constellation of cherry-colored moles shining on her forehead. Their hands waved in the air. Jan, afraid of waking the family, kissed the image of his beloved and placed it on his heart. He also picked up a stone from the path; finally, he turned and continued on his way. The puppy, glued to his legs, followed behind in a cheerful trot. Jan knew he should chase the dog away with stones, but he couldn't bring himself to do it, so instead he tied the pup to the bridge's rail. At the last bend of the river, as the water struggled to flow under the sheets of ice, he heard the whining barks of the animal merge with the forest's heartbeats.

One never forgets a smell, just as one never forgets a touch nor the way things were when one last saw them, and this wounded memory stars in the migrant's dreams for years. Sitting on the ship's deck, studying the sea, or trying to identify constellations, Jan would retrace those final moments until they became sculpted in his memory. He can almost paint a picture of Ruth embracing a tearful Anastazja, helping her into bed between sheets he never shared, tucking her long blonde locks away from her face, drying her tears, bringing her an herbal tea. He also thinks of Ruth's loneliness when he finds work and Anastazja joins him in America. He imagines his mother dining alone, his books on the table; finally, he imagines the village without him.

Along with nostalgia, the journey has surprises in store for him: a man with fully black skin, small boats carrying fragrant fruits, the bracelet with blood-colored beads that he bought for his fiancée, crowding into the hold like cattle when it rained, the indescribable feeling of loneliness blended with a longing for the future. In a few weeks he saw and learned more than he had in his whole life in the village. At night, lying dumbstruck under the sky's dome, he dreamed of Anastazja and America. America and the Statue of Liberty holding her torch; America and its skyscrapers, asphalt roads, zealous automobiles, men dressed in suits. America, its unintelligible language and unknown neighbors; meeting his father's brother, working in the bakery, searching for a bed and a table where he could set down the blanket his mother had gifted him, the stone from the path, the young lady's portrait.

No one on the ship spoke Yiddish or Polish, so Jan Siedlecki could only communicate through hand gestures and a rudimentary training in dance. He mimicked some words in Spanish and Italian, although he didn't quite know what they meant, and, to avoid sinking into a depression, he began playing with the little ones: between them there were no barriers, so he was able to rediscover the joy of communication. In the evenings, when the migrants made music, he understood two things: that these cheerful sounds only masked the heartbreak, and that the frenzy of dance was the only cure for the sadness that threatened to drown them all.

The sunsets, identical to one another, painted the ocean with a red never seen on his mountains. The only break in routine was the dreadful storm that forced everyone to crowd into the ship's hold, where Jan held the children in a melting pot of fear and vomit; thinking, as he consoled them, about the children he would have with Anastazja. He counted the weeks by carving notches in an oil barrel, but the journey felt monotonous, an excessive amount of time to spend crossing the ocean. To kill time, his mind would return to Anastazja, her body's warm touch, her profile in the window. Then he would reread the last postcard his uncle sent, running his finger over the vague ink: "You'll see the Statue of Liberty standing over the Hudson River. Then the ship's siren will sound. Then you'll go down to the pier, and I'll come find you."

The birds that had trailed the ship for days no longer seemed anxious for scraps, the migrants had gathered their belongings, and a bubbling anxiety was brewing on deck. One morning the siren launched its moan, like a whale in heat. In the pale dawn, the ship switched on its lights, like a cluster of stars, and began circling a wide estuary larger than all of the barley fields Jan had ever seen. It approached a port where haughty ocean liners and diligent cargo ships slept. With the early morning air hitting his face, Jan let his anxiety show through. But there was no statue to be seen, no Hudson River, no city lined with skyscrapers; just a huge and unintelligible sign, a massive iron bridge, a landscape as flat as the sea, a bleeding sunrise, and an ecstatic pier simmering with affection.

Alone with his luggage, Jan filled with anxiety, then indecision, and finally with a terrible weariness that soaked his waiting hours in fatigue. When the pier grew deserted, he accepted his fate and started walking. It would take him a long time to realize that traveling to America could mean docking in New York, but also in Buenos Aires. And so, after wandering for weeks, he stepped into a bakery that needed hands, began to knead until the veins in his neck swelled like cords, and slept, worn out, on the sacks of flour. Despite not receiving a wage, he wasn't in need of shelter or food, and as such he began to consider himself a lucky man. This was more, much more, than what winter in Poland had to offer.

One afternoon, watching him skillfully shape the dark bread that sold so well, the owner of the establishment asked the head baker: "Who is this young man?" "A Pole, sir. A Jew." "What's his name?" "I don't know, sir." "How much is he being paid?" "Nothing, sir. You never told us to pay him anything."

From then on, he received a daily wage, bought a suit, sat for a photograph to send to his fiancée, and finally found a room with a bed where he could lay his mother's blanket and a table where the stone from the path and Anastazja's smiling portrait could rest. The room was in a kind of tenement house then referred to as a "conventillo." It had formerly served as a brothel, and, to remain in good standing with God, Jan called the rabbi, who gave him his blessing; after all, who could turn down affordable housing. Five years later, Jan mourned the death of his mother; after six years had passed, he had enough money to call for his fiancée. He had built a small house on the outskirts of the city, and even though it was a long commute to the center, he grew vegetables in the garden, cared for two clucking layer hens, and could respond to his neighbors' greetings with a reasonable handle on the language. In addition, he was highly regarded in the bakery, where they admired this lonely man who thought only about work.

As he dreamed of Anastazja and measured his progress, Jan also felt the pride of having been faithful to his promise. On Sunday afternoons, when he was off from work, he would go out and walk around the deserted city. And while it was true that his young manly urges had led him to sleep with many kinds of women, it was also true that he had never kissed any lips other than Anastazja's. Those affairs were a simple sinking in and pulling out, losing his memory and emptying himself, but nothing about that pleasurable embrace could displace the memory of his fiancée. So, one of those Sundays, after leaving an unnamed bed and taking a stroll around the skyscrapers in the city center, for the first time he sat in a bar on Calle Corrientes, spent however much a glass of wine costs, and filled himself with the courage to write to the young woman's father asking him to send her to be married. The next day he brought the letter to the post and attached a money order for her passage. Soon after, he received a date and the promise that his future wife would meet him at the port of Buenos Aires.

Jan used the time between the receipt of the letter and the ship's arrival to decorate his little house. Ashamed of its state, he bought a large bed, linen sheets and towels, a frying pan and a pot, a beveled mirror, and a rug with an inextricable pattern that he deemed worthy of a palace. He came to an agreement with his neighbor that his fiancée could stay with her at first, since it would not look proper for them to share a house before marriage. He went to the doctor, and, from that moment on, abstained from dealings with other women. He asked for a raise at the bakery and the owner, now aged, promoted him to manager. And just like that, diligent and cheerful, the eve of her arrival came. Afraid of oversleeping, he stayed in a boarding house, where he placed his ironed suit on a chair. On top of his trousers, he rested his shining straw hat. He could barely rest. He set off early and hardly ate breakfast, his stomach in knots.

In the long hour that separated him from where the ship would dock, he walked through the city that emerged in the dawn, crossing paths with the occasional car. He was the first to arrive at the pier and waited there studying the horizon, as alert and determined as a watchman. He had already lived what happened next. Slowly, those receiving the travelers filtered in: noisy Spaniards, Jews dressed in all black, contractors jingling the keys to their estates in their hands, lone men with flower bouquets, ladies in elegant hats awaiting their friends.

In the crowd, Jan reminisced about his own arrival, the lonely daze of the first months, the nights before he had a bed, the nonsensical language, the immense and alien city where his confusion ambled and where—he now understood—he had a place. All of his sadness was fading away; he was a migrant full of dreams come true who, despite his unfamiliarity with some of the local customs, wore new shoes and had a home where he could welcome his wife. Anxious and aroused, he fantasized about having Anastazja next to him; then he imagined her in the synagogue in her bridal gown, listening to the seven blessings, and he trembled envisioning her lying naked in his arms; he pictured how life would be when their dreams came true in this booming country. He was broken out of his trance by a sudden restlessness in the crowd, which, like a clamoring animal, seemed to stir in unison from the morning's slumber. In the distance, the ship was a speck of light on the glowing horizon. A joyful wail rebounded off the docks. Soon after, the collective elation shattered into hundreds of distinct stories.

When no one was left on the pier, Jan Siedlecki—his bunch of flowers now withered—remained, waiting for his fiancée. The peaking sun produced a sticky heat, and his new suit, which had made him feel so assured in the early hours of the morning, now stifled him; seagulls shrieked with a metallic sound that struck Jan as sinister. He fanned himself with his hat. Confused and disappointed, he was about to return home when a woman wearing a bizarre coat stopped in front of him, set her luggage down on the cobblestones and began speaking to him in the accent from his village. She was very tall, taller than he was, and she had a remarkable demeanor. No one had spoken to him like that in years. Hearing the melody of his language, Jan saw the closed shutters, the path that led him away, and the ice sheets flash before his eyes. He smelled fresh bread and heard his dog barking. The memory grew so defined that it finally rounded into an image and resolved the enigma. The woman standing before him was sturdy and had dark hair. She had taken off her hat, and a small constellation of cherry-colored moles shone on her forehead. She was talking hurriedly in a strangely childlike voice; then she began to cry, and Jan thought she might be about to kneel. As he stopped her, and she blew her nose with the handkerchief he lent her, she stammered an explanation for her journey: how her father had ordered her to go, how he declared, badgering her and anyone who would listen, that she was a much harder sell than her sister—much more beautiful and easier to marry off—and how their mother, instead of taking her daughters' side, had also insisted, to keep up appearances, that the youngest daughter's wedding could not come before her older sister's, under any circumstances. Then, between hiccups, Ruth pleaded that none of this was her fault; she never wanted to travel, she didn't even want to marry, and if he decided to abandon her right now, she would understand completely. Then she began to sob with such anguish that Jan took the huge woman's arm and brought her home.

Before long, the war broke out and the beautiful Anastazja, along with her parents, disappeared on the way to some concentration camp. Jan did what he had to do: though he never stopped loving Anastazja, he married Ruth, and they were as miserable as two married people could be. They both spent what was left of their long lives adoring the beloved fiancée, the dearly departed sister, by means of the portrait that rested on the cupboard. They had only one son and one grandson, both of whom would be named Jan. Nothing remains of the couple but a portrait that a photographer obsessed with bridges took of them by chance. In it they appear aged, him waning, her ever larger, each standing on opposite ends of the railing, both absently gazing towards the horizon, as if they were strangers.

Gold Coins

MY FATHER tells me how he crossed the ocean with a bag of gold coins. He hid them on his back, like an atrophied bone, and the constant pressure forced the coins into his skin like a branding iron tattooing the king's profile. He also brought a well-bound book, a quill and inkwell, two clean shirts, and a bar of soap. Examining these belongings, those on the ship mistook him for a member of the clergy and didn't say a word when they saw him reading; this saved him from the sailors' childish brutality. It was barely halfway through the 18th century, so he was one of the first to arrive and make a fortune. No one wanted to settle in this savage land. A good convert, he was courageous and shrewd in business dealings. With the bag of coins, he bought twenty thousand hectares on the banks of the Paraná River, in the heart of the barrancas, a feral land as vast as time itself, where there are no olive trees, where the ground is not made of burnt clay, where no structures stand, save for the tough grass where cattle graze.

There, where the land peers over the jungle, the jungle peers over the river and the river, bloodied with snakes, sinks into Brazil, he built his first home. My father lifts up his shirt so I can run my finger over his perfectly round tattoo. "Go on, touch it," he tells me, and I feel the hollow of his back like a raised trophy, solid and woven with muscles. I can't see his face, but I see that minted mark charring his skin. Then he went to the port and hired settlers to work his land. "Monkey faces"—he calls them—"piranha teeth." I listen silently to the crackling embers, the heron letting out its plaint, the frogs croaking in the lagoon. My father runs his tongue over his teeth and continues: "I filled the land with five thousand wild cattle. A rodeo with five thousand cattle. Do you understand? A whole day wasn't enough to count them. At night I would calculate how many I could have after the first hundred years. They can reach a billion"—he said— "if I survive. Do you know what a billion is? If you start counting your breaths now, by the time you die you still won't have reached it." Even when I was older, the impossible pit of numbers gave me vertigo.

When my father stopped caring about counting his money, he decided to build a house to accommodate the books that, just like the livestock, were multiplying exponentially. He also married that woman who was a Spaniard like him, the one with light-colored hair and eyes. Then he told himself: "No, a house won't do—I'd better build a palace." His wife's pale and childlike foot fit in the palm of his hand, but her fist was strong and resolute, and with it she struck whoever came in the way of her whims: my father adored these despotic ways. When the palace, with its fifty bedrooms and ten bathrooms, was finished, he erected the turret that overlooks the river and in it installed the library. His wife looked out the window, grimaced and said: "Yes, it's all very nice, you have your books, but look: the park is savage. I want violet flowers." And then: "I want peacocks." A week later, she repeated: "Golden flowers." Now they're blue, like sunset in La Vera. My father sent for bulbs from Holland, which rotted on the ship; holmoak sprouts that rejected the dense soil; conifers with piercing roots that managed to take hold. The same boat carried lacquered furniture from China, marble from Greek quarries, beaten bronze to be used for the balustrade. And the house grew under the watchful gaze of his wife, who turned out to be a fierce administrator. Upon her death, the peacocks took over the garden with their cries of mourning, their tails fanning the fields to be divided between heirs.

In the turret overlooking the river, my father started to write, closing the window in spite of the jungle's greasy heat to remove himself from the peacocks' cries. "I was successful," he says, "very successful—my portrait still hangs in the Academy." He goes quiet and seems to have fallen asleep; I stroke his hand. He doesn't notice me, and his cracked skin offers no reassurance. I'm young, and I think of the children I will have, what they will think of all this. Outside a strange silence has fallen; a cow moos, hundreds of calves respond nostalgically: it's weaning season. Moths buzz and trace spirals around the light fixture, striking each other and rebounding off into the night. From time to time my father moves and smiles; sometimes he breaks down in groans. I try to remove my hand but end up trapped for hours.

When I wake, he's talking to himself, as if the long night hadn't cut his monologue short. I make no effort to understand him; stroking his hand I discover the profile emerging and gaining mass in the dawn, and I feel a certain sense of affection, like that of a mother towards her capricious child. He speaks in French or English, on and off in German, scanning a Babelian clutter of ideas, his sentences falling in a dust cloud of rhymes; he loses himself in his hodgepodge of anecdotes. He smiles, his lips smooth and curved. "My wife," he says, "my wife." He is referring to the second one: the most capricious, the most beautiful.

The park had matured by then; the disheveled palms stitched the horizon and the lovely oleander flowers, scorched by the heat, vomited their venomous fumes. Sometimes at sunset he would stand quietly by the window, studying the river and its silver curves. Then he decided to travel. He had come from Europe, and to there he returned with a full hold. He makes the sly gesture of someone who counts his money. "The King of England welcomed me"—he says—"I crossed the channel to Paris in a deafening airplane." He launches into a sinister laugh and then tears up; he always whimpers a bit talking about this trip: how they named him ambassador, how it took two servants to button his suit. And the endless jewels for his wife, the Flemish paintings, the sculptures. "Houses are like wine," he says, "they have their moment, their splendor. This house soured after my journey." He sniffles again before continuing. "No one who's gone on this trip comes back the same; it was much more of an adventure than the war." He also says, "I've been alive for many years, but this is the only thing that truly happened." I look at my father in shock, realizing that none of him happens in time. He doesn't talk about the violence, the iron broom that swept over Europe; he only talks about art, precious objects, leisurely walks along the river. I arrived late to this life, I think to myself, late to this vigorous existence that only flows backwards. "And our mother?", I ask him in anguish: "Do you remember my birth? My siblings'? Do you even know the names of my children?" He stares at me with empty eyes. As I cover him with a blanket, I see the coin-shaped scar, now stretch-marked. It's almost noon and a cool breeze is drafting in, which could be harmful for him; the multiplied peacocks are fighting over food, devouring the garden. He wraps himself up, half smiling, and studies me. "You don't look like her," he says. "You don't look anything like your mother." Then he adds, lowering his voice as if it were a secret: "You know she was crazy, right? She made me as happy as a man could be, but also utterly miserable. Good thing she died leaving enough time for me to marry my mistress."

Once again it's night, and he still hasn't eaten. I go to the kitchen, where my father's latest wife has left a plate with some vegetables. I'm about to bring it to him when I hear him shouting. He's calling his wife, crying out for her; hers is the only name he remembers, the only thing that remains from his prodigious memory. I approach slowly, dragging my feet, supported by my cane, and stroke his head; I tell him she's coming home soon, not to worry; then I bring out the food and his voracious appetite calms him. I'm an old woman, void of cares; the only thing that worries me is what will happen to my father when I die. Nothing remains from the old palace; the walls are empty, the gutters clogged, and insects now weave their millenary lives in the baseboards. The park has relinquished its trees, the livestock has been sold, and the peacocks devour each other; at night, in the hideous silence, the scent of the oleander flowers is all that echoes. There's a poet who says that to extend man's life is to extend his agony and multiply his deaths. He is mistaken. I see how my father strives for something so palliative and basic as food. I, on the other hand, have practically stopped feeding myself in old age, and I have forgiven him for everything. Even for when he dipped his toes in the blood-filled pool. I speak to him of the soulless empire of the beautiful. He claims not to remember anything; with his mouth full he shouts over my questions, demanding his wife. I don't tell him that she rarely comes by anymore, that she's too busy selling the scraps, that her sons now own the palace, and that some nights I hear them shuffling around the north wing, dark like bats. Instead, I insist that he shouldn't worry; everything is fine, we've reached the billion cattle, and, when he's able to walk again, he can look out the window and see, pecking around the park, the peacocks with their iridescent plumage.

Cold

A PALLID sun scales the horizon. Birds of prey, hungry and fierce, trace spirals in the sky. The mother turns to protect her son, who's straggling behind in the snow. Watching him makes her swell with pride; he'll survive the steppe's dry wind, the winter that is waning. He'll make a fine chief one day, leading the group to safety; he'll take the best females for himself. Along the ice, which is starting to break, the river's torrent cheerfully flows; blades of grass emerge stitching the shore. Already a troublemaker, the calf strays from his mother and falls back in search of sun and food. He doesn't want more of the lukewarm milk that curdles in his stomach; he's ready to try out his new teeth. He's at the edge of the riverbed when he stumbles. Down the dark and slippery clay slope he slides, unable to regain his footing. He kicks and fights to free himself but sinks down even further. Mouth and eyes full of mud. In his lungs, the foul smell of mire. He looks to his mother, who is trumpeting in a craze, begging the rest of the herd for help. The last thing the calf sees is the sky.

Later, under the yellow glow of night, a shining mound surfaces from the mud. The female sees it, launches an infinite howl, then at last turns and follows the herd of mammoths towards the north, to summer pastures.

The Siberian permafrost is full of these beings in eternal slumber who have stayed almost perfectly preserved under the ice, and whom the villagers consider gods of the underworld. Not much of the landscape has changed since the ice age; the air is more humid, and the sky has lost its electric hue. Saber-toothed tigers no longer roam, nor do woolly rhinoceroses. And the leafy grasses and shrubs that once fed them no longer grow.

Out of all the buried gods, out of all of those bones and skulls, the native peoples favor the baby mammoth hidden beneath the mound of mud shaped by spring on the riverbank. Yuri knows that he is not to be awakened, for it would bring terrible misfortunes to the group. Not like the misfortunes that came with the discovery of gas, which is now being taken away from them along with their land. Nor like the misfortunes that came with the introduction of alcohol, which has turned them into drunken rabble-rousers. Yuri knows he must not tell the white men about his findings, about the enormous tusks pushing through the thawing ice.

About the bones along the coast that have been stripped bare by the wind. He must not mention the little, sleeping god. If they find it, he thinks, they will come and sell it like they do with everything, even though it's not made of ivory. If they find it, he tells himself, tragedy will strike. At night, Yuri rests beside his family: five girls from his first wife, five boys from his second—a train of little ones who were born in pairs and triplets, like litters of kittens. He likes the scent of the reindeer hides spread across the floor; as the snow wafts down outside, he savors the herd's stench by the stove. Snow is falling and everything is white, like a dream. At night, Yuri dreams of the little god. He's become widowed once more and is not sure if it's wise to marry again. The tent won't fit more offspring—it's impossible to move for shepherding with so many people inside—but he's still a spirited man. During the long winter, he's started looking at his eldest daughter with lust, which frightens him. Lyuba is a very pale girl with an extraordinarily beautiful feline face and sharp little teeth, but a scar crosses her lip. She cut herself on a sled blade trying to help him one snowy afternoon. The mark doesn't make her unattractive; rather, it gives her a strange smirk. She spurs the dogs on as well as the best shepherds, and in winter she accompanies him to the southern taiga forests. In summer they travel together to the Arctic Circle to forage for cracked lichens to feed the animals.

Although she has not yet turned twelve, the woman in her is emerging; at the same time, she has the strength of a man. And she also dreams. Like her father, she dreams of the god. Maybe this is why Yuri trembles when he looks at this mirror of himself, of his strengths and weaknesses. Watching her sleep, he feels the crude urge to lie down next to her, to smell her feral scent up close and touch her. But he reminds himself that he's her father and prays to the burial mound, asking for advice. If he stays clean, if he doesn't drink, if he doesn't hit his children and gets his work done, if he keeps his distance from Lyuba, then the child god will reward him with a revelation. The revelatory dreams appear three nights after he has taken his vow of purity. When the beings of the underworld stand before him, when they summon him, he feels an obscure bond between himself and the little god. He obeys, even when the signs compel him to abstain from women or urge him to sell his best stud to his enemy. He obeys and stays silent; then he goes down to the river, where he sings a lullaby to the baby mammoth, to the god with milk in his teeth, until he goes hoarse.

One night, he dreams that it's all over in the Yamal Peninsula. It's not a comforting dream; it's awful—he sees spring melting all the rivers, where hundreds of animals are groaning awake. Animals in their icy bell jars, struggling to free themselves. Immortal animals awakened by dreams of death. Along the landscape, which has stayed identical throughout almost forty thousand years, machines with enormous jaws emerge and chew the ice. Yuri, unable to sleep, peers out the tent's opening. Outside, nothing has changed, just the expanding albino plain. He's calmed by the monotony.

Nothing is dreamt in vain, nor prophesied without reason: nothing that happens in the future avoids leaving its trace on the present. One week later, a foreign couple appears at the child god's burial mound. She is tall and blonde and seems unwell. He must be her husband. With a few ill-spun words in Yuri's own language, the man explains that he's just a photographer who has come from far away to capture the wonder. Various men from the village are standing next to the couple counting money, and in the midst of all of them, indifferent, surfaced in his icy crib, lies the god, now turned on his back. Yuri sees all of him for the first time, just as he dreamed, and the scene strikes him as such a flagrant disgrace that he can feel something breaking in his chest. The god from his dreams is hideous and precise; he can even count his teeth and eyelashes; instead of a joyful trunk, the god bears an appendage with the likeness of an old man's limb. He appears fragile, made of parchment; the only thing missing is a chunk of ear torn off by some modern dog. There is hardly any dignity in his twisted mouth, where anguish and death braid together. So that's what it was: that was it. Yuri feels like crying. First out of sorrow, from the loss of mystery. Then because he has become orphaned, and then from the shamelessness of it all, for the god's naked-ness also stains him with infinite disgrace. As they load him into a wheelbarrow, Yuri notices that the god's skin is crack-ing. He also sees his childish face, blind, frightened and piti-ful, his halted walk with twisted drunkard knees; finally, he watches how they carry him off, swaying.

Without saying a word, he lets them photograph him with the beast, and, when no one is left, he heads back to his tent and vomits. Then he takes off his clothes and lays down on the furs by the stove; emptying a bottle of vodka he studies his naked body, which seems to be covered by the mammoth's pebbly skin. It's very late, and maybe it would be better to forget everything—fall asleep and search for some comfort behind closed eyelids. But the god no longer exists, and Yuri knows he will never dream again. As the sun rebounds off the horizon, he waits for Lyuba to arrive. The girl greets him, then becomes frightened by his brutal gaze. Before she can open her mouth, he strikes her so she can't scream; holding her down, he tries not to look at the scar on her lip, covering her face so her large steady eyes cannot watch him.

At last, worn out, he too cries—mourning the misfortune of this tainted land.

Madison County, The Bridges of

RATHER THAN staying seated next to her husband and holding in her desire, as the film recounts, in that tense moment, stopped at the traffic light in the rain, the woman gets out of the family pickup truck, runs through the rain, and climbs into her lover's car. She offers no explanation to her husband, nor does she have time to leave a letter. Nor can she say goodbye to her children, who are still young, but everyone knows the power of desire. She has made the right choice. The moviegoers, who were anxiously holding their breath, let out a sigh of relief. They like this new ending to *The Bridges of Madison County*, and with their dose of romanticism left intact, they leave the cinema.

Beyond the cameras' gaze, away from the spotlight at last, the woman sits in the passenger seat. She lets the photographer put his hand on her shoulder, and, just like that, their journey begins. It's been days since she met her lover, but enough time to desire a life together; he's awakened in her body the certainty of passion and the echo of a dormant youth. And she's not just any woman. Years ago, driven by the same, uncontrollable fire, she left Italy to follow and marry a soldier. He was an American hero, and she, without hesitating, agreed to be the wife of a good man and move with him to a farm in the United States, where their two children were born.

She turns her head and sees him fading into the distance—that soldier no longer in uniform, turned farmer without the sheen of adventure. She feels guilty, though not excessively; after all, who could resist the call of passion? Her lover now rests his hand on her knee.

She doesn't have luggage, so before catching the plane in New York, he buys her clothes for the journey. They're beautiful clothes, different, and the woman feels like she has shed her skin. Now she's another person: younger, more elegant and graceful. As she explores the city, he takes photos for *National Geographic*, visits libraries, introduces her to more people in two days than her husband has in all their years of marriage. She's pleased to have coupled with this internationally renowned photographer, feeling like his fame is contagious. She is the lover of an artist, a bohemian, and when he embraces her in their hotel room in Tanzania, she can feel herself floating. Sleeping under the veil of the mosquito net, awakening to the lion's roar, playing the role of a female waiting for mating season, peeking out of the tent to find sunrises that look like embers, wading across rivers that burst into waterfalls, seeking shelter from torrential storms, reviewing the images over and over again until she finds the best frame, assembling foreign delicacies into dinners for two, traveling without a fixed destination.

After some time she has seen twenty countries, hundreds of sunsets, thousands of faces. And her lover, in an homage to the day they met, has photographed the bridges in every city. One is stuck in her memory. It's a photo of an elderly married couple in a Buenos Aires park, each one gazing off in the opposite direction, as if they were strangers. The image of an old park taken over by peacocks also weighs on her. In her rare moments of rest, in some lost hotel, she writes to her children. She never hears back from them and blames it on her constantly changing address. This pains her, but her lover says it's best not to dwell.

One day she wakes up with a bad feeling in her gut. They're in northern Russia, interviewing a reindeer herder who, in the endless snow, has discovered the corpse of a mammoth. It's a calf, frozen in the same position he met his death, curled up like a frightened child. She feels sick and returns to the hotel, sensing that instead of finding the prehistoric animal, she has stumbled upon her own agony. It's a frigid sensation that makes her shut herself in the bathroom and vomit; it feels like she is wrenching ice cubes out of her stomach. In the evening, taking advantage of her lover's absence, she calls her old household, and as the phone rings, she imagines it on that same table with the runner she crocheted, next to the floral armchairs, the lit fireplace and the sheer curtains pulled open. She imagines it in that life where nothing ever changes. She yearns, how she yearns to speak to her children. She also wishes to talk with her husband, ask him how he is. But no one picks up. That night she sleeps poorly.

Much like the ice that concealed the mammoth, something has broken inside the woman's heart. She no longer gets the same joy out of traveling and feels lonely when her lover leaves her in the hotel – sometimes for weeks at a time – to arrange photographs, go over his bookkeeping, organize interviews. For a while now she's also been his secretary; everyone remarks on the brilliance of this passionate couple. "How romantic!", they exclaim, when he tells their story in public, and they eye her with envy, as if she were a heroine.

One day he informs her that he has to go cover a story in Rome. The woman is overcome with emotion. She figures that now she can return to her mother's house and will finally get to speak to someone from her past. She's nervous throughout the whole trip, which, due to his commitments, is weeks long.

She takes advantage of him having an important meeting to take a bus to her old village. Everything has changed. In the same place where time had sowed poverty and war destruction, there are now lovely villas, vineyards, hotels.

Her mother hardly recognizes her, but they embrace until it hurts. "You've changed so much," her mother says. She also says, "You look beautiful." The woman prefers not to respond; her mother is now an old woman. Later, when they settle down, she invites her into the house; sitting facing one another, they take each other's hands, looking at one another without knowing what to say. Finally, her mother blurts out: "I'm so sorry, dear." She's surprised and asks why. "I heard about your husband," she says. "He was a good man." This is how the woman learns she is a widow, though her mother doesn't know which illness ended his life. She tells her that yes, the children do write to their grandmother once in a while; they seem to be doing well. She shows her a photo. The woman feels that her life, her real life, is spread out on that table with the vinyl tablecloth, in that house she left centuries ago to follow a man. She wonders what would have become of her had she chosen a husband from the village, had she settled down there. She thinks of the infinite possibilities contained in a life. She also thinks about those children of hers, who look like strangers. She doesn't say any of what she is feeling out loud and arrives back at the hotel on time, so her lover doesn't ask her where she's been.

Although they stay in Rome for several months, she doesn't go back to visit her mother. She's lost weight and it suits her; she attends receptions that are ever more luxurious, and her lover's fame precedes her. He is almost an old man now, and she is almost a young woman; the years separating them have become more pronounced. Nonetheless, his body still arouses her affection, though she wouldn't be averse to someone younger. An opportunity arises and she takes it but leaves the affair feeling bad about herself. "I mean honestly," she thinks, "the young man sleeping next to me is probably the same age as my son."

Sometimes she remembers how she and her lover used to embrace under the bridges of Madison County. Other times, she remembers the baby mammoth. At times, she remembers the elderly couple from the bridge, torn apart by life. One day she receives a letter: it's from her children. "Dear Mom," they write, "we're older now, and we'd like to see you. We're not angry at you—we just want to talk about our dad. My brother and I are wondering how such a simple man could have held so much passion. You knew him well; you can help us answer this question. As we were going through his papers, we found this envelope with your name, enclosed here." The woman unfolds the paper, where a single sentence reads: "I will always love you." Sometimes she wonders if she made the right choice getting out of the car on that rainy morning. When the question stings her, she tries to scare it away, as if it were a fly.

Silence

For María Luisa and Omar Ramos

"What if I put out my eyes at the same time? . . . That way
we would both belong to the same side of the world. . ."
—Ismail Kadare, *The Blinding Order* (Trans. David Bellos)

A HAND, the old man says, and he grips the collar of the dog trying to run down the platform, after the red-haired girl. He checks his pocket watch: it's exactly ten to seven in the morning, the same time showing on the station's clock. A hand, he repeats, and he sees the girl stepping onto the train. As the cars gather speed, the hand waves goodbye, cutting through the air. The hand of this girl who is fading into the distance is like the hand he saw back then, the old man thinks, a hand waving goodbye at the same hour, when the day is just starting to emerge. Almost a child's hand, its palm facing up, the fate line carved, innocent and open, as though trying to see if it's raining. For as long as he lives he will never forget that hand, waving from the train, on that winter morning all those years ago. It's summer now, and the girl waving goodbye brings him back to that cold dawn. He is now an old man who nobody notices, but in those days he worked as a switchman and wore a shiny uniform. Back then, like today, the day was just showing its colors, and he came out of the booth wearing his uniform and whistle. The gold watch was new, a gift from his wife; he liked to close the case with a resounding click at exactly 11 minutes to seven, one minute before making the required signals for the snorting train to enter. He had raised and lowered the levers, laid the tracks. And left the station sign without a speck of dust: Angoulême. At that very moment, the locomotive roared into the station, bursting with energy. Back then train tracks were cropping up everywhere like silver streets, perforating hills, piercing tunnels, shuddering in front of factories. The switchman felt like he was a part of all this progress; he had just gotten married, and it was hard for him to pull himself away from his wife in bed in the mornings, disentangling his legs from hers, detaching himself from her arms. He would ride his bicycle to the station and, upon entering the office, he would pour himself a steaming cup of coffee from his thermos. Everything was perfect. After the twelve o'clock train he would return home, read the newspaper in his armchair. How he would have liked to lie back down with his wife for just half an hour, take a nap together. But duty was duty.

That day it was six thirty in the morning. He kept an eye on the time and got into position on the platform. Then something strange happened, because he heard the sound of the train's engine a few minutes before it was scheduled to arrive, and any break with routine meant that something was wrong. The train made its entrance, stopping so the driver could stretch his legs, the switchman gave the obligatory wave, and out came a stranger. It was a freight train, and the cars smelled rancid, like no one had cleaned them in a long time. The switchman felt ashamed, because anything related to the railroad was his responsibility, so he walked towards the stranger to take it up with him. The man, seeing him approach, jumped back into the driver's car, without waiting for any order. Then what happened happened, with all those people on the platform. When at last the train started to move, he saw the hand waving.

It was nothing but a hand, a hand floating in the air, he tells himself, just like the one belonging to that young woman with the red hair who just got on the train. He brings his leg closer to the dog's warmth, petting him on the head.

Now that he's seen the train stop at ten to seven, like he does every morning, he can return home. He's a widower, but this is of little importance to him. His wife's death came long after she had left him, when he hardly remembered her, when, in fact, he had already buried her. There are many ways to die, he thinks, and some happen while the heart is still beating.

So at first he was alone within himself, then he was alone in his house, then in the bed he shared with his wife, and finally even his body became foreign, drawn onto the green armchair, and the air he breathed seemed strange, like it came from a different planet. That was when she, tired of trying, decided to leave. At least that's what she said: "I'm tired of trying." It wasn't because she didn't love him, she made that clear; she still loved him like the day they met, she said, the day they met. It was that she was tired of waiting for him to talk to her. "When you know what you want to say, write to me," she insisted, suitcase in hand. "I'll come back. But don't ask me to take care of a man whose words have left him."

The switchman looked at her incredulously: he had been trying to talk to her for months, but everyone knows how strange women are.

It was because of the silence. And because of the dolls, which she never forgave him for. He still has a picture of his wife on the mantle, a smiling young woman in a floral dress, her hair gathered into two braids. It was taken a long time ago, centuries back, before the war, when trains were innocent. It was from a time when he would still embrace Madelaine with his chest of metal muscles stuck to his bones, with the prestige of his switchman uniform and its shiny buttons. But what he had told her and she didn't know how to hear wasn't something inconsequential, something that someone could hear and still maintain a smile and her dress and the scent of bread. It was something immense, almost impossible to face, a wound that multiplied like dead leaves and stayed within, crackling in a bonfire.

The truth is that Madelaine liked the shiny buttons on his uniform and his youthful embrace, but not the words he whispered to her that night. First, with that governess attitude she had been showing lately, she told him: "Don't get yourself mixed up in trouble. You didn't see or hear anything, understood? You're blind, deaf, mute." Then, when he continued, she put a finger to his lips; she didn't sit by his side ready to listen. No, she didn't do that. She just stood there smiling, undaunted, and finally started chatting again about nothing. And so he carried on with burning embers in his guts and she carried on with her routine, until the switchman stopped talking.

Now, sitting on the bed, the old man paints a mental picture of the red-haired girl from today's train. He takes off his shoes, tosses them to the side and lies down fully dressed. It's hot, his brow is coated with watery pearls and his hair is stuck to his forehead. If it weren't for the sweat, he might seem to be dead. An hour later he's woken by the dog, locked in the kitchen, scratching the door, trying to get out.

Madelaine was the daughter of a wind-up toy manufacturer. She had grown up among little animals that spun in circles or played the drums, and she piled her collections all around her. Watching her cook, the switchman would admire the precision of her movements, fruit of her meticulous upbringing. She was cheerful, affectionate, and she had accepted him from the start, even before he got down on one knee and she, looking down at him, said "yes." Of course, in those days he was an excellent catch—so handsome, and with those shiny buttons.

The first night she didn't want to undress, and he had to wait almost a month for her to let herself be touched. He held out but didn't tell anyone, lest the whole town doubt his manhood. It was after their trip to the city, when he bought her a floral dress and a straw hat. After having a drink, they had gone to the photographer to sit for a portrait. In the photograph, Madelaine was holding the hat in her hand, her two dark braids gleaming like a foal's rump. That same night she let him hold her, and right there, with an expert certainty, she let down her hair and brushed it out in front of the mirror; then she took off her nightgown and stood naked in front of him, saying: "Make me a son."

She didn't say "I love you" or "it hurts" or "be gentle." She didn't even blush. It was an urgency, a command, something she seemed to have thought about for so long that it was implanted in her womb; the switchman was so taken aback by her tone and the words she said that it was all he could do to comply. Then, when he came out of his stupor, the dam of his desire burst, flowing into the body that sucked it in. And that hoarse voice in his ear, insistent. "Make me a son."

In the morning he woke up later than usual, happy and relaxed, and he heard Madelaine cleaning the house. She didn't say anything, didn't come kiss him, didn't stray an inch from her routine. And like that, a new ritual was established between them. He would rise very early, ride his new bicycle to the station in his shining uniform. They would eat dinner in silence, she would clear the table, and when they got into bed, again the disquieting "make me a son." It happened with the precision of a wind-up doll, the old man thought, and he placed the monkey dressed as a soldier playing the drums in front of his wife's portrait. He wound it up and let it reach the edge of the dresser, where the little animal, blind to all limits, tumbled off.

Madelaine didn't just collect brass toys and clockwork mechanisms; she would accumulate anything: match boxes, thimbles, pincushions, and especially dolls. In the mornings she talked to them, grooming them like children, ironing their dresses and sitting them in their designated places: dolls with glass eyes and long eyelashes, natural hair and pink painted cheeks. Myriam, with her blue bow, always sat on the armchair next to the fireplace. Marie, dressed in frills, sat on the shelf among the collection of coffee saucers. Muriel was on the green velvet armchair, and Margot, the favorite, was on the bed.

Margot on the bed in her baby outfit with her papier-mâché smile. A strange model, practically a collector's item, her rotatable head was covered by a bonnet, leaving half of the face always hidden. Laughter or tears, tears or laughter. The switchman never learned why his wife chose one facial expression over another, nor what message, if any, she wished to convey to him. Margot had a mechanism on her breast that meant that, when she was shaken, she would emit a sinister cry.

All of Madelaine's dolls had names that started with "M," as if they were merely variations of a single identity. He could live with them all and ignore them, except for Margot, who, sitting atop their quilt, tortured him, reminding him of the child who was still to appear. When Madelaine started grooming them, to avoid getting angry he would grab the hoe and go out to the garden, the only space where he was not infertile.

The old man looks out the kitchen window. It used to be decorated with ribbons and flowers, now the glass is dirty and the garden deserted. Out there, he piles up the garbage he never gets around to throwing away.

Madelaine didn't like him hanging up laundry in the garden. "Bring it inside," she would tell him, muttering: "The neighbors don't need to know what we wear inside, what do they care. Don't be foolish, cover it with a sheet," and she would reprimand him in the tone one might use to scold a child. Of course, that made sense because the garden was a beauty, its furrows quivering with fertility, its expectant plum tree. The only thing hanging on the clothesline was his jacket, like a shiny flag. In the mornings, Madelaine would help him button it up. Then she would wipe his bicycle down with a wet cloth until it was gleaming and say, "get a move on, you're going to be late." He would ring the bell so all their neighbors would know that he was leaving his house early to fulfill his duty, even though he had a beautiful wife.

By his side, the dog is wagging his tail, trying to lick the old man's hand. He opens the door and lets the dog out onto the patio to fill it with joyful barking.

"Quiet now. Tomorrow we'll go back to see the trains. You liked the red-haired girl, didn't you boy?"

He sweeps around the table, picks up the wind-up figurine that has fallen on the ground and, without giving it another thought, tosses it into the trash.

It was awful what was going on at the station those days. The switchman didn't know German, but after listening over and over again, certain phrases stuck in his mind. The soldiers would shout them at the men getting off the train, shivering, their hands in the air, to everyone else's dismay, although later no one would speak a word of it. He saw and heard not only shouting and barking, but also the sound of bolts unlocking, cars opening; they went from car to car asking *wie alt? wie alt?*, a question normally directed towards a small child while patting his head, *wie alt?*, how old are you?, and to those over the age of ten they said *raus raus*, they barked *raus raus*, and instead of patting their heads they forced them off the train with the butts of their rifles, so violently that the men couldn't even say goodbye to their families. Some women howled like wolves. Others, terrified, seemed to have fallen mute: it didn't matter, sometimes silence and shouting are one and the same. The switchman saw everything, standing on the platform in his shiny uniform that suddenly began to seem absurd. It was all absurd, the uniform, the cap, the watch, the station and the bread he had eaten for breakfast. Absurd, his bicycle, the nights spent with his wife, the wind-up toys. And there he was, the whistle between his teeth and a lantern—it was a foggy morning—making the regulation signals.

They would make the men get off, as well as the boys over ten, and then they would stand there on the platform, with their arms raised, sometimes for hours, until another train came along to take them away. As the train disappeared, everything seemed to be wrong. Silence howled, speech was blinded: hell had opened its eyelid for just a second only to close it once again.

No one wants to remember anything these days, the old man thinks, but all of that happened in plain sight. And, as the convoy faded away, the shards of a shattered world paraded before his eyes.

No, he didn't cry. After seeing all that he didn't cry, because men don't cry and also because, at a certain point, pain becomes mute. He rode his bicycle home at the usual time, and the first thing he did was close the door and window and tell Madelaine quietly:

"Madelaine, listen, I saw something"—and he held her hands so that the secret would seep through their touch, their veins, their blood. Madelaine listened to him solemnly. And when the words had filled her ears, she withdrew her hands, got off the bed, smoothed the quilt and said:

"I've got chicken for dinner."

At first the switchman thought that she was trying, out of the gentleness of her heart, not to upset him further, and so he also kept silent. They would talk later, when he smoked his daily cigarette and she took out her knitting. But that night, Madelaine turned off the light earlier than usual and immediately went to sleep. The next morning, without straying from her routine, when he tried to speak, she put a finger to his lips:

"Shut up, you fool," she told him, "What could you possibly tell me that I don't already know. . ."

He waited like that for weeks. At night, when she would throw herself at him again with her usual passion, he tried to reciprocate, but everything now felt as mechanical as raising the lever to lay the train tracks. It was a silence so dense that it vibrated in his eardrums leaving him deaf, just as before the screams from the train had left him blind.

The truth was, it was no secret that the Germans had closed off the Les Alliers camp and taken the Spaniards away. Where and why? These were questions that no one asked. And the neighborly conversations over hedgerows continued, as did the small talk with tourists in the station, the superficial jokes between coworkers, the perfectly ironed switchman uniform, the bicycle at the ready. The only difference was that everyone was hiding behind a mask now glued to their skin. The days passed like this. The only thing thriving was the garden, and the engineer dedicated himself to battering the earth to get the rage out of his system.

It was more or less around this time that the rebukes started. His father-in-law, the toy manufacturer, had given up those trifles and was now engaged in an ill-defined activity that was making him a lot of money.

"A boy, I need a boy," he insisted. "Look, I only have this female"—and he would point at Madelaine with pride and contempt at the same time. "I need a boy to carry on with all this when I die"—and he said "all this" in an abstract way, his hand signaling to a darkness that extended much beyond the room.

One day, the switchman accompanied his father-in-law to the doctor because the old man's nail was oozing pus. The doctor looked at him, turning his head, before prescribing an expensive treatment.

"If you don't do what I say," he stressed, "it's going to get infected, and you could lose your hand."

The man looked at the physician with his greedy gaze, thought it over a bit, seemed to make some mental calculations, and finally spat out:

"How much to cut the finger off?"

This was the man to whom he was to deliver a grandson?

The only one who didn't seem worried was Madelaine. Her chest was plumper than ever, her hair shiny. Her personality was also changing. Now, when she saw him working in the garden, she would shake off her apron and cross her arms, like a matron waiting for an unruly child to come to his senses. The switchman, confused, barely dared to look up and would keep on digging, in the hope that she would get bored and go back into the kitchen. But Madelaine could stay planted there for hours, tapping the earth with the tip of her shoe.

What if he accepted that there are things for which there are no words? He was ready to exchange his misery for everyday matters when, that same Friday, in came the women's train.

It happened one morning almost at dawn, the old man remembers, a morning not unlike this one, when a red-haired young lady got on a train at Angoulême station and stuck out her hand to wave goodbye to a dog; a milky, pallid morning, but in winter, not summer, and so many years ago, with a gloomy sky and the river groaning under sheets of ice. It snowed so much in those days that people couldn't leave their houses; he would take the shovel and Madelaine would watch him with pride; any woman knows the value of having a man to shovel snow. He kept doing what she asked him to do, even more now in winter, when it was impossible to dig in the garden; he obeyed so he didn't have to face those frozen eyes. By then, people were all too aware of what was going on, so that even conversations at the bar or with coworkers became evasive.

The worst of all wasn't the contact with the Germans. Not because they were more or less awful or evil; some of them were practically children. What was truly sinister was the way that, through repetition, the most serious incidents became banal, boring, and everything started to seem normal. In some parts they talked about those trains in the way one might discuss soccer, as if it were something bureaucratic, dull, common. Everyone knew everything, the old man thought to himself, even though years later they claimed that no one knew anything.

In a sense, there was nothing to complain about: the trains went along at full speed on their studded iron plates, his switchman uniform was shining, and the schedules had returned to normal. The only difference was that certain trains were rigorously guarded. Everyone paid their fare, as it should be. Some paid as they had done all their life, at the ticket window, of their own accord, choosing the departure time, the seat, the destination. And others paid involuntarily, with what was confiscated from them. It was a logical system: since the passengers in the special cars didn't want to travel, their will didn't enter into the equation in any way, so they couldn't choose the time, seat, or destination. Indeed, the railroad and the tourism industry made a fortune in those years, because those who were taken to the concentration camps in cattle cars also paid their way, and thus the trains experienced a boom, a moment of unstoppable growth.

To understand what people mean when they refer to these trains, one has to imagine fear embedded in more fear embedded in yet more fear, an unforeseeable anguish, the sound of the train striking one's brain, the asphyxiation in the cars, the vertiginous outlines packed together like bodies, time being crushed, and in one's eyes splinters, traces of a caress, fleeting objects, the dust of things. And that hand, that young woman's pale hand floating on a winter morning.

It was like a cage of screams in the ghostly dawn, screams as white as the snow rebounding off the train. The old man doesn't remember the month, but he remembers the cold, and the layer of frost covering the world. The switchman had already adopted his first puppy, a white German shepherd who used to rub against the man's legs and sleep at the foot of the bed. Madelaine protested and tried to drive him away waving a pillow and hissing like a rabid cat. But the puppy, hiding underneath the bed, would wait for her feet to rise and, when the switchman was sleeping, he would stealthily approach to lick his hand. Together they would go to work, the puppy trotting behind the bicycle, barking happily at everyone they passed, and in the station, the switchman would pet him on the head to feel something alive, something warm when those trains approached. It was easy to distinguish them, not only because they carried people in cars meant for cattle, but also because of the stench. Despite the snow, despite the cold, the switchman had never smelled anything like it; who knows where these people had traveled from and what was going on inside the train. That morning's train was full of Spaniards, that's why it caught his attention. What were they doing there? Later, he discovered that they were being transported for a specific purpose: to build the Mauthausen camp. But what about the women?

He saw the women on that liquid morning, after the men were dragged off and they were left alone in the car, too frightened even to scream. The switchman was waiting there with the signal flag in his hand, wearing the shiny jacket that Madelaine had recently ironed, that absurd jacket, ready to give the departure order. Then he was struck by the intense gaze of a beautiful, slim young woman. Beautiful and silent, her long hair filthy beyond belief, with two big dark eyes like the Virgin in the village church, with no tears in those striking eyes even as they dragged away her father, a strong man who was clinging to her, but the Germans forced the two apart with their rifles. A Madonna of the morning, in the snow. And the worst part, the switchman told himself, the worst of all was that she wasn't crying. She wasn't crying, the switchman thought, his gold watch in hand, and as he said it, he felt a hot tear streak across his cheek. A tear from him, a man who never cried. The young woman had already been shoved onto the train and, for a few moments, everything was silent; even the snow that, slowly, was falling. As the men remained on the platform with their arms raised—dark silhouettes against the white snow—and the train started to move off, the young woman who wasn't crying did something simple and poignant: she stuck her hand through the planks of the cattle car and waved goodbye, as if she were a tourist leaving for summer vacation and planned to see him again, in a week or two, to catch up over an afternoon tea under the linden trees. Just like the red-haired girl from today, the one with the big eyes said goodbye with her hand, a thin hand with tapered fingers that little by little were lost in the distance. Meanwhile, the tear rolled down the switchman's cheek in slow motion. It wasn't summer like today, it was winter, and the switchman held in his pain; he finished the morning without listening to anyone, unable to process the rattling terror of that cage of screams, tightened to exhaustion.

Some weeks later, he encountered the women's train again. They were returning from who knows where, but he no longer saw that hand; no one was talking about the train full of women whose men had been torn away from them, who wandered like tourists because they had paid their fare, accidental tourists, accidental victims who would end up who knew where. This time he saw them drag away a sick, dirty, cadaverous woman for fear she would infect the rest of them, they said, as if illness were the problem, as if the plague wasn't the one they all carried in their souls. Indeed, everyone was infected with death. Or fear. Or indifference. He waited in the station to see what they were doing to the women, he waited to find out why they kept coming back, he waited until they carried off the sick woman, he waited to see, once more, that intense gaze: but those eyes didn't appear, nor did the hand waving hello or goodbye; all that appeared were the stench and the screams, this time somewhat weaker.

From what the sick woman said, they learned that this train did not have a destination. This was also evident from the itinerary; the train had been making the rounds between concentration camps, stopping at each of them to see who would take charge of killing those women, playing "yes or no" with them. The train would strike the gate, asking the wardens who came out with their dogs for permission to enter, whether it was worth the hassle to load the women off the train. From Angoulême to Mauthausen, from Mauthausen to Ravensbrück, from Ravensbrück to Berlin, from Berlin to Paris, and then back to Angoulême, the switchman saw them for a second time before losing them forever, it was like a riddle for children, now you see me, now you don't, cities with tongue-twister names, a merry-go-round, a violent refrain that made the hinges of the machines groan, repeating, "fear of dying, dying, dying, dying." Then the switchman, with a rock in his throat, returned home to speak.

The only one there was his father-in-law, who had shown up with a crate full of food; the shortage seemed to have gone into effect for everyone but him. Shortly thereafter, Madelaine appeared, dressed like a little girl, her arms full of parcels.

"Why are you home so early? What's going on?"

She took off her boots, shook the snow off of her coat. In the bedroom she opened boxes, smoothed papers, put away linens, passed her hand over the immaculate quilt, picked up Margot, her doll, her baby, rocking her back and forth to make up for being away so long. Then she turned the doll's face to its crying expression. Without saying anything she grabbed her husband's jacket, shook it off, sunk her face into the fabric and sniffed it before hanging it up on the coat stand in the entrance. His father-in-law was sitting in the green armchair, smoking one of the few cigarettes to be found at the shops and looking up at his son-in-law from the newspaper as if he were a stranger who had just sprouted up there, before turning back to his paper. Lying on the coffee table, Muriel with her porcelain smile seemed to be laughing. Madelaine had sat down in front of her father, as if she were his wife, and was knitting a little scarf for Margot, whom she settled in her lap. Margot watched him with her icy little eyes.

The switchman shut himself in the bedroom. A little later, when he heard the door close, he peered out into the living room. No one was there, nor in the kitchen nor in the cellar. In the frozen garden, the furrows formed a tiny mountain range. He made a cup of tea before taking the wheelbarrow to go fetch the dolls.

An hour later, Madelaine was sobbing in her father's arms. Through the frosted windows, she saw her husband warming his hands over a bonfire, she saw the inky smoke rising towards the sky, she saw the molten and sticky papier-mâché bubbling, she saw the shattered porcelain, the cardboard skeletons writhing, the hair burning like torches. Margot, with her little bonnet, had already burned, her face halfway between laughter and tears. Muriel's eyes were hot and floated in their sockets. Myriam, in her little blue dress, lay on her back, her feet caressed by the flames. Then the switchman threw into the fire the pillow from their bed, the sheets, and the quilt where Margot had cried and laughed for so long. When it was all over, when the switchman's hands were no longer red from the fire, he took a shovel and dug up the remains of the pyre of bloodless, naked bodies, the mountain of corpses; with the skill of an expert gardener, he began striking the earth with the hoe, burying the smoke and the ashes.

Can the dead fertilize new life? Can silence? Does everything cultivate and achieve meaning—does everything have a purpose? Indifferent to these questions, the puppy, white as snow, let out joyful barks and danced around the embers.

A long time has passed since that bonfire. As he walks towards the station, the old man thinks of the secrets brought by the trains from the East, from Poland. Rails that speak, he thought, gusts of words that spin in those metal wheels; nothing is secret in the world of trains. He recalls the rumors around town, the fear that those who had been liberated from the camps might return, the blind persecution to which they were subjected just when they thought they were free, persecution that was no longer at the hands of the Germans, but rather at the hands of ordinary people. He remembers how, when it was all over, normal people pushed the Jews from the trains; they pushed the people leaving the camps off the cars without anyone telling them to, without anyone threatening them. It wasn't the Germans, it was good people who pushed the Jews to their death on the tracks, on the side of the road, abandoning them there, like animals.

Good people who live shut up in their homes, the old man thinks to himself as he strokes his dog; people who distrust their neighbors, count their money and don't care about anything else, good townspeople. And his father-in-law's hand with its fierce greed, Madelaine's crazed dolls watching over everything. Decent people, like that smiling young woman in a flowing skirt holding her son by the hand, that baker carrying a basket full of fragrant rolls, that man who stops his car to let an old woman cross the street: good people.

And that floating hand that says goodbye forever, waving in the dawn, the slight hand of a woman who is leaving.

So This Was Love

For Mercedes Calabrese Obligado

FOR SUCH an old man, he had these shining eyes that seemed to want to say something above all the tubes and medical care; his smirk also caught her attention. He used to be quite famous, his niece said, before offering her much more than people normally pay for this sort of thing.

"I want him to be taken care of, but I have two kids and a ton of work, and I don't even live in the city. I'll drop by from time to time—I've got no choice but to trust you."

Lyuba was given keys and instructions. Truthfully, this was her first time taking care of someone. She had tried to make a living teaching Russian classes, but no one wanted to learn Russian in Normandy; the Russians were the ones who paid to learn French. Besides, she wasn't blonde or tall, but petite and flat-chested with Asian features.

She adjusted the old man's pillow, and for the whole afternoon, sitting next to the window so as not to waste electricity, she studied for her exams. When the night nurse arrived,

Lyuba had already gotten used to the old man's eyes. Where she came from, they would put the old men who had no woman to care for them on dogsleds and take them to forage for lichens. Her grandfather had died helping her father with the reindeer, and her grandmother had survived more than a hundred years without ever taking a break from her cooking. Everything was different here: Lyuba needed money, she was too old to live under her adoptive parents' roof. Initially she had fantasized about returning to Russia, but the cliché of adopted children searching for their past didn't make sense with someone like her, who remembered everything. Besides, she wasn't even Russian—she was a nomad, an inhabitant of the Arctic.

Jan was waiting for her under a streetlamp that cast a stream of light over his head. His whole body was covered in tattoos and he kept his head shaved, but those innocent eyes revealed that he was less wild than he liked to let on. Lyuba was attracted to him, although proximity to men produced an almost pathological fear in her. She met Jan when she had just arrived, in French class; they were the only two who spoke Spanish, and it was almost obligatory for them to become friends. He walked over to Lyuba and held out his hand; she let him walk her home but didn't invite him up to her apartment, though she waited as he finished his cigarette. It was more than Jan had achieved the week before, so he waved goodbye and left feeling pleased. He liked this girl, he really liked her; just seeing the small scar above her lip made him tremble.

In the morning, the old man seemed to receive her in better spirits. He couldn't speak, but he strained his face into a grimace that resembled a smile. And then there were his eyes. Overcoming her disgust, Lyuba washed him, grateful that he wasn't staring at her as she rubbed him down with a towel. He was an old man with glass bones, but he must have once been strong and handsome—no doubt blond— with light and inquisitive eyes. Curiously she didn't reject the task, she thought; it's better this way, it was in her best interest to keep this job as long as possible. The night nurse, before leaving, had advised her not to get attached: "these old folks don't last long," she said, barely concerned that the sick man could hear her. When Lyuba finally spread out the blanket, the old man brushed her hand, and she thought she saw a grateful smile. It wasn't bad, she told herself; this job, in spite of everything, wasn't bad, she just had to take care of the sick man who, in any case, spent most of the day sleeping. After feeding him, she was also sleepy and lay down on the loveseat next to the bed, her book open on her belly. She woke up because the old man had started striking his cup with a teaspoon.

She was late to the last class. Her gift for learning languages filled her with pride. First the language of her village. Then Russian in the orphanage, Spanish with her adoptive parents, and now French. She didn't speak badly at all, barely with an accent; in fact, she spoke much better than most of her peers. Jan got there even later and sat behind her. He shyly stroked her hair in greeting. Lyuba pulled away slightly, but didn't withdraw completely.

A week later she had settled into a routine. In exchange for the old man averting his gaze when she bathed him, she would let him refuse food without making a fuss; the old man had enough trouble keeping himself alive. Sometimes she would sit by his side and sing him those songs she learned as a girl, ones that no one could understand here in France: songs about snow and hunting, songs to pitch a tent or accompany the dead. The old man listened as if he knew them and, if Lyuba stopped, he would come out of his trance by furiously striking the cup.

One morning, instead of the nurse, she found the niece.

"You're doing a great job, Lyuba," she told her, looking pleased. "Why don't you show him some magazines, or these old albums? I'm sure he would like that; he used to be a very renowned photographer, some of his pictures are famous. Take what you want from these piles and show it to him, maybe it'll calm him down, though the poor guy barely understands."

But that wasn't the case at all. When Lyuba brought her slender hips close to the old man's ribs and opened a magazine on the bed she could feel him tremble, as if his blood, stupefied by time, were recovering its intelligence. And when she started turning the pages back and forth, she would note a slightly sticky warmth where their sides met: pictures, pictures of all kinds, feature stories, faces, cities. And bridges, lots of bridges. Sometimes the albums and stacks of magazines were so heavy that she had trouble carrying them, so one afternoon she asked Jan to help her organize everything. This seemed to upset the old man; he hit his cup without her being able to calm him down, only quieting when Lyuba stroked his head. It was a rough, bald head, punctuated with what was left of his hair, along with moles and scabs. Although she knew him all too intimately, she had never touched him gratuitously; this was new, and it made the wrinkles on the old man's forehead suddenly slacken. Lyuba held back a smile: the old man still liked women.

He's found a rival, she sensed, and the idea amused her. Just like reindeer, men competed against each other until death. That night she dreamed of a mammoth calf trapped in the ice. It was a recurring dream, and she knew its appearance meant something.

In the morning she arrived slightly late and the nurse complained because she had had to wash the old man, who got cranky and spat out his breakfast.

"I gave him a sedative," she said, "and he's calmed down now, but you can't imagine the punches he was throwing into the air—how could a dying man hide so much strength?"

Although he must have heard her, the sick man didn't open his eyes. Only in the evening, when the street was dyed pink, did he signal for her to bring over the albums and magazines. Lyuba opened one that exclusively had portraits of women; many of them were with the photographer who now, in the fullness of his age, seemed attractive: in Buenos Aires, in New York, in Tanzania, then several photos featuring a blonde woman with soft features: he had been a worldly man, a bon vivant, and here he was, sniffling before his ashes. Lyuba adjusted his pillows and turned off the lights. The old man seemed to be crying, and in an almost maternal gesture she held his hand in the darkness and stroked his arm. She felt his brittle skin—on his forearm there were several wounds from which a mess of blood emerged. She had the feeling that the old man's soul was wrapped in tissue paper and that, underneath all these obstacles, desire still throbbed. She treated his arm, bandaged it again; it got late, and when she went out to the street, Jan was in a bad mood, smoking his fourth cigarette, and he met her grumbling. That day they parted almost in anger.

At night she dreamed of the mammoth again. Now the ice and mud that covered him were cracking due to a trace of heat, and, next to the animal, curious onlookers swarmed like ants. It was such a vivid scene that she woke up crying, her father's violence so close, so close. Jan was also there, although she couldn't remember what he was doing in the dream. She got up, her body aching, and spent the day slightly shaken, avoiding the old man's eyes. She didn't bring him the photographs, she didn't stroke him, she ignored the spoon against the cup. As if repeating a mantra, she filled her head with irregular verbs in French, conjugating them in all the possible tenses, from top to bottom, bottom to top, until her brain was empty. She declined Jan's invitation to go to the movies and didn't let him walk her home. She felt that she was being unfair, but she needed to be alone. Finally, when she got home, she climbed into bed, covered her face with a pillow and a dry sob, as if made of stones, reduced her to crumbles. She had never cried before. Not even when her father disappeared in the snow, not when they were rescued and she was taken to the hospital to treat her wounds and her siblings to who knows where. She peered out the window. Spring was sprouting, and on the still-frosted roofs the last icicles dripped: the thaw had begun.

She was awakened by a shower of pebbles against her window. It was early morning and there was Jan, waving at her, freezing to death, wearing few layers as usual, his head shining under the streetlight, steam spouting from his mouth. When he looked up, Lyuba was touched by his wide smile. They ate breakfast in near silence, and as they walked down the empty street, Jan put his hand on her shoulder. Shivering, Lyuba thought: "He's going to kiss me." Then she was horrified by her own fear. But Jan limited himself to walking her to the old man's house and, with a nervous smile, said he wanted to talk to her—maybe tonight, he pressed, he'd come pick her up for class. Lyuba walked up the stairs and stopped on the landing, almost choking, before she realized that she had hours to calm herself down; she could barely breathe when she greeted the old man, and he hit the sheet indicating that he wanted her to sit by his side. But today her routine was of no use. The old man hardly let her wash him; instead, he ate more than ever, his surly expression replaced by the smile of a capricious and ravenous child. Like a premonition of what was later to come, halfway through the morning the niece called to tell her that the night nurse had a fever and begged her to stay. Then she added,

"Just for today, Lyuba, it won't happen again, I promise, I'll pay you double. But you'll have to make do by yourself, I don't have service in the village."

Lyuba said yes almost without thinking; the emergency freed her from her date with Jan, she was calming herself down by reading when the old man started to rattle the teaspoon; then, with her mind blank, she surrendered herself to her job as if it were a narcotic. She was turning the page on the fourth or fifth magazine when she saw it. There, in a worn-out photo, turned upside down, was her father's god. The old man seemed particularly happy, as if the image filled him with pleasing memories. He pointed his warped finger at one image and then another, and then another, until

Lyuba came to understand that he was the one who had taken them. He and that blonde woman who went everywhere with him. It was him. She was taking care of that old bastard whose pictures had caused their misfortune. And that was it.

Without making any movements that might arouse the old man's suspicion, Lyuba kept turning the pages of the magazine; when she managed to calm down, she called Jan and tried to keep her voice free of any undertones. Then she promised him that of course, when it got warm she would go with him to the beach, she heard his happy and assured voice—yes, I'll go with you, she repeated—she was willing to promise anything because nothing mattered anymore.

As she prepared his medications, she tried to focus on what her ancestors would expect of her, but in her brain, cottony and emptied of ideas, nothing seemed to stick. She fed the sick man, who was now exhibiting the whims of a capricious child. Avoiding his eyes, she fell asleep on the loveseat, exhausted. She dreamed of the mammoth again. In her dream, the god of the underworld, still cowering under the ice, opened his frozen lips and mouthed: re-venge. Revenge against that old man, that dying man who didn't know the half of the damage he had caused with his stupid photo. Revenge.

Lyuba studied him in the half-light. The way he was lying, asleep with his mouth ajar and his arms on his stomach, he already seemed to be dead. Frankly, he only had a little further to go: a pillow held down with force, a higher dose of medication, an air bubble leaking into an IV, an opened window that lets in the cold. It's so easy to give an ending life a push; who would bother to investigate? Wouldn't the niece feel liberated? By killing a man under her care, her ancestors could rest in peace, and she could think about love. Love: that which is rarely known to a woman who has been raped. She opened the window: the whole night was before her.

She was broken out of her trance by a peculiar cough. The old man had opened his eyes and was staring at her with a frightened expression, his eyeballs yellowish and bulging, his skin very pale.

"Don't do it," he seemed to be saying. Don't do it.

She tried not to look at him, but his gasping breaths filled the room; she turned her back, and, shivering, kept peering out the window, focusing on stars that looked like clouds of flour, and she stood like that until startled by the sound of the cup falling onto the parquet flooring.

"I shouldn't turn around. If I'm going to kill him, I can't let those huge eyes trap me."

But, before the thought drove deeper into her mind, Lyuba went over to the bed, and, mechanically, pulled up the covers, adjusted his pillow. Then she looked at him. This was her enemy? Disoriented, the elder eyed her as if she were a stranger: his death had begun.

Perplexed, Lyuba understood her situation. She didn't have anyone to call, no one to take charge of those tremendous hours; in the profound intimacy of death they were alone. She looked at his body, his eyelids pressed shut in a mixture of abandonment and fear, his hands like claws clutching the sheets, as if the soft white fabric could save him from ruin. To which gods would he pray? There was no one on the walls or in his photographs, no one to hold on to for some solace. Lyuba felt a wave of pity flood the scorched hole in her chest. It was a watery, almost essential tenderness. Where was her hatred? Her thirst for revenge? No, none of that was left: it had disappeared along with the dream.

She sat beside the old man and started stroking his arm. But the old man, instead of calming down, flailed around, trying to fill his lungs with the little air he could catch; he was fighting, clinging to the last threads of life, it looked like he was tumbling, drowning in mud. Lyuba understood, then, the only thing she could do to soothe this strong, lively old man who was now dying. Very slowly she took off her blouse and let him see her delicate breasts, let him caress them with those rough hands as no man had ever done before. Then, when the sick man seemed to be worn out, she lay down next to him and let her young warmth bring him solace. And when she sensed that he was calming down, she whispered in his ear:

"Don't be afraid, don't be afraid. Let yourself go."

As she pressed him against her chest, the old man contracted and then seemed to relax. Lyuba felt the life leaving him, and before hideous death could peer through, she closed his eyes and covered him with a sheet. Then she covered herself as well.

The city was emerging in the light of dawn. Peering out the window, Lyuba could see the last traces of the Milky Way's giant circle repeating in a spiral, orbiting over everything. She went to the kitchen and made herself a coffee. As she warmed her hands on the mug, she told herself that later on she would call Jan, she would let him kiss her.

Black Holes

For Martín Obligado and Natalia Ares

A MAN is sitting on a park bench. He feels a sudden pain and, as he falls, he touches his chest. It's humiliating to crawl, his pants stained with dirt; he's so hunched over that he can't cry out, unable to reach his pills. It's his second attack, he knows it will be the end if no one helps him. Suddenly, at eye level, he sees two polka-dotted shoes, like the ones flamenco dancers wear, red stockings, and the rolling hem of a little red dress. A girl holding a balloon approaches and studies him. She doesn't understand why this man is squirming on the ground; adults are so strange. She's about to call out to her mother when a pigeon comes so close that she thinks she can reach it. She's always wanted to catch one of those birds. A few days ago, her older sister brought home a chick in a box, and they hid it so their mother wouldn't see. It wasn't a pigeon chick—it was a sparrow with a yellow, needy mouth—but she spent hours rubbing it in. If she were to catch this pigeon, her sister would have to swallow her words: "stupid," "midget," "flea." This pigeon with its iridescent neck and round little eyes, with its curved and proud beak. As though trying to provoke the girl, the bird takes a few steps, opening her wings to launch into flight; it's just a bluff—she waits and scrunches her wings because a male is approaching. They chase each other cooing, it looks like the male pigeon will catch up to her. The girl turns and runs after the birds who, at her abrupt movement, take flight with the sound of distant clapping. She runs after them and lets go of the balloon, which is the last thing the man sees, swaying in the air, before he closes his eyes.

Elsa peers out over the balcony. She sees a red balloon rocking against the blue sky. A clear morning is shining; she's longed for one of those since she moved abroad, a clear morning, like the ones from her childhood. Autumn must be starting already in Madrid; here one feels like cheering on the early spring. It's a feeling that comes with her return to familiar ground, to the neighborhood, to the jacaranda tree teeming with sparrows, to the view over the quadrilateral Plaza Irlanda. The park, the hollering, the children. Two pigeons stop on the ledge and coo at each other. It's so hard to talk about spring without sounding corny. She recalls a verse: "It was the flowering season of the year." Góngora? Yes, Góngora, and those disorderly Baroque-era poems that needed to be organized, read from one side and then from the other, diagonally, pieces of a magnificent puzzle searching for their place.

It's almost magical being here, in Buenos Aires, on this balcony. Her husband had a conference in Mexico and evidently didn't want her to accompany him. More and more he prefers to travel alone, and he has a point: dental prosthetics conferences are anything but fun. Besides, their marriage is, at this point, predictable and monotonous, though they don't verbalize it for fear of hurting one another.

"When we retire," he said before leaving, "then we can go wherever we please together. Without the kids."

When we retire. That blessed phrase kept dribbling like a ball. When we retire. She had never thought about it before. First, because when you move to another country you lose ten years just obtaining the bare minimum. Then, because the kids were so much work that she didn't even have time to think about the future. And the future had arrived—it could be summed up in a single sentence: when we retire. That's when she started making her own plans.

Madrid in the summer is suffocating; surely someone else wanted to cross the world and reach another hemisphere, where it's winter. She mentioned it to all of her friends, her colleagues at the library, but the price of plane tickets and the economic crisis dissuaded the few people who didn't yet have plans. So she called her son to invite him:

"Not-a-chance, Mom." And Elsa imagined him brushing a lock of hair off his forehead. Then he sweetened his tone, "What if you invite me for dinner? I have something important to tell you."

She hung up the phone feeling sorry; no matter what he told her, the trip to Buenos Aires was decided.

As she gathered her papers, she judged that she still had a few cards left to play. It was upon returning home that she thought maybe it wouldn't be such a bad idea to invite her youngest, but then she had to admit that she didn't like traveling with her; where her brother was perfect, the girl only tried to bolster her personality by using her mother's as a doormat.

What the hell, she said, I don't need anyone to go with me on a journey to the past—because ultimately that's what it was, without a doubt. I'll go alone. As soon as she verbalized it, she realized that she had not been alone in the last twenty years. That's when her niece wrote to tell her that her childhood home was free.

"It's changed, but I think you'll like it. There's still the tree and the Polish-owned bakery. The old folks died; I think their grandson runs it now. Do you remember the bakery? That huge woman who never learned Spanish?"

Of course she did—how could she forget—Elsa recalled it instantly with the precision of olfactory memory: the soft bread on her way to school, the giant woman always dressed in black, sweeping the sidewalk, that constellation of reddish moles on her forehead.

Now she's here, on this balcony: "It was the flowering season of the year": Buenos Aires in September. Everything is repeated and out of place at the same time. If the old Góngora still filled her with passion, if the old house still came back to her with the neighborhood's scent, why not call Fabián?

It wasn't spring but summer, and so many years ago. Graciela was nervous and a cool breeze ruffled the back of her neck, beaded with sweat. With her hair up she looked taller, her pants fluorescent green; she always wore green to accentuate her red hair. Sharp hips, platform shoes, a black t-shirt with an ample neckline, a little skinny perhaps. The bus sped; she got on as it was practically moving. As they drove past Plaza Francia, a man pressed up against her pants and started rubbing himself. Disgusting. Finally, she was able to slip away towards the door and, reaching campus, she realized that it was too early.

Too early for what? To feel what she was feeling, surely. Fabián had only asked her to get coffee before class. "To go over our notes," he said. Nothing about dates or furtive glances, nothing about loaded sentences or casual touches. Clearly, he had a girlfriend. Fabián had a girlfriend, Graciela repeated to herself, she had even seen them together on campus: a small girl, reasonably pretty, physics student, with a melancholy expression and a braid down to her waist. He had a girlfriend and her name was Elsa. But even though she knew that much, there was Graciela getting her hopes up, always falling in love with the wrong person. The breeze perked her nipples. Covering herself with her folder, she walked towards the bar, surveying the occupied tables through clouds of cigarette smoke. Fabián wouldn't sit too close to the front—he was shy. Nor too far in the back—he didn't like to go completely unnoticed either. She parked herself in front of the door, staging the scene so it would look natural, but when she opened her notes, everything looked blurry. In the bar's entrance, a pigeon clucked in pursuit of crumbs. She hated those winged rats and shook her folder to scare it off. In that moment Fabián appeared.

"Fanning the air?" Graciela smiled crookedly, stammering:

"The pigeons. . ."

"You're bigger than they are, don't be afraid, silly"—and, without any warning, he stroked her hand.

Now she felt her arm hairs bristling. Would Fabián notice? She stared at his hand not knowing what to do, and when she raised her eyes, Fabián was peeking at her notes, unfazed.

At night, reviewing the facts for the umpteenth time, she told herself that it had been a coincidence, a simple display of affection between classmates, a protective motion; none of what she was feeling had any logical grounding. Nevertheless, she dreamed of Fabián.

Summer took people away: caravans of young people migrating after their exams, sweaty and firm bodies fleeing to wherever the air would blow. Seeing as her mother was more and more unbearable, Graciela tried to spend as little time as possible at home. She didn't have any more exams; all the time in the world was on her hands. All that time, and the empty summer where Fabián had vanished.

She bought a low-cut green dress and kept it in her wardrobe, along with some very tall sandals. She cut her saffron hair almost like a boy. When it got so hot that going outside became impossible, Graciela would try on the new clothes in front of the mirror. Then, if the coast was clear, she would gaze at herself naked and, caressing her body, try to pretend that those hands were not hers, but Fabián's.

One day, tired of herself, she called him, but when a woman picked up the receiver, she found herself unable to speak.

Finally her parents left for the beach. For the first time, she refused to go, and, also for the first time, they let her stay home alone. Sitting in the chaos of her room, Graciela made two decisions: the first was to find a job, and the second was to lose her virginity before school started. That afternoon, bored out of her mind, she decided to squeeze herself into the green dress and go out on the prowl.

Luckily, Elsa's mother didn't force her to wear all black and let her stay away from those bleak festivities where the women, with their freshly styled hair, talked in low voices and neurotically drank coffee. The only thing that gave the room a bit of happiness was the huge stained-glass window. Elsa had always been baffled by women's urge to run to the hair salon the day after someone died: to the salon after the death of her grandparents, after the death of her younger sister in that accident she hardly remembered, to the salon now, after her father. The phrase struck her: after her father? Is there a before and an after, or does everything last? It doesn't last, you idiot, of course it doesn't: your father is gone. Gone.

She left almost fleeing from home. Her father had died, yes, she wouldn't see him again; it was hard to accept, even though she had seen him suffer so much in the last few months that she had wanted it all to end. Outside, the dense summer had turned the air into a purée. She looked for a phone and called Fabián. His sister picked up.

"Did you call a little while ago and hang up?"

"No, that wasn't me."

The spoiled younger sister. Minutes of silence to show that she was at her mercy:

"Should I wake him?"

Yes, wake him, Elsa felt like shouting, how can he sleep when I'm dying of grief? But instead she said:

"No, don't say anything."

Death and the black void. Its dirty footprints. Its filthy dirty indelible footprints, its muddy boots sullying everything. Death. Hideous death. Did everything die? Would she die? Would her story with Fabián also die? A balloon vendor brightened up the evening. Elsa bought one; after a while she didn't know what to do with it, and she let it go. Seeing it go free, she felt like she was turned upside down, like she was the one moving off into the distance, swallowed up by a black hole. Surely this is how her father had gone, gravitating in space, and they would collide again at some point in the huge spiral of the universe.

She decided not to go home until night, so she walked into a bar. Like always when she was depressed, she binged on sweets thinking about her father. Then she ordered a beer. Her father and her little sister, and her grandparents, all together, like molecules of a single mass, peacefully floating towards who knows where. What was it all about? A collapse? Time crystallizing? Was it all, in fact, simultaneous? Ah, that voice, the persecutory voice surging from the dark magma, that echo in her head:

He's gone, Elsita. He's just gone.

Elsa was a physics student, the only girl in her class, very at odds with the views of mom, who wanted her to have a reasonable future, and very in line with the views of dad, who accepted her as a continuation of his own eccentricities and kept a series of gadgets in the basement that he assembled and disassembled in almost sacred rituals. The two would hide there, conjuring up the sadness of the house:

"Look, Elsita, the time machine"—and he showed her a device that looked an awful lot like an egg beater. "If I beat really quickly, we'll travel to a black hole, and there time is different, Elsita, it's different—there all human beings find each other again. If we beat hard enough, we'll find your sister."

It's hard to dismantle the beliefs we held as children, Elsa thinks, those faiths without fissures, far from science's pragmatic verification. The whole egg beater and black hole thing was absolute nonsense, but they had so much fun sitting on the same bench, their eyes closed, turning the crank as hard as they could. Indeed, hugging her father, she felt time slowing down, and matter itself; her arms weren't long enough to grab his torso. It was so nice to feel him close, only for her. Without realizing it she murmured, "Dad," and her eyes filled with tears. Had he replaced her by now with her dead little sister? Were they having fun together? She imagined them immersed in time's relativity, falling through a tunnel, holding hands. She was a bit tipsy. She silenced the voice with another beer, drank two more and saw, to her surprise, that the evening light had been devoured by night.

She set off walking down the avenue. It would be crazy to walk all the way home, but she didn't stop. No, nothing dies, nothing fully dies. Reaching the park, she was frightened by the path without a visible end; she was judging whether to take a taxi when two strong hands grabbed her by the waist.

"I caught you!"

"Fabián! Weren't you at home? Your sister told me. . ."

"At home? I haven't been home all day. My sister's an idiot."

Elsa looked at him the way someone would look at a ghost, then brightened. As he stroked her head and brushed the hair out of her face, playing with her braid, she felt that the best thing that could happen in the whole world would be for Fabián never to learn anything about death or disappearances, for him to keep being that normal guy with the big, bright eyes that inspired trust. They had been dating for two years, and Elsa had always known that they would end up married. Though married was an excessive term, more like living together. She couldn't imagine her life without Fabián.

Sitting on the plane, Elsa recalled the year her father died, that horrible year that took her away from school and forever away from physics. It was a summer day from how long ago, thirty years? She got home late, having spent the night with Fabián in one of those hourly hotels that Buenos Aires is full of, and in the morning, as they ate breakfast and made plans, they vowed eternal love for each other. Eternal love, Elsa smiled, a love that lasted barely a few months longer, until Fabián traveled to work on a project for his degree and she received her father's inheritance, which enabled her to take charge of her future.

Is that why she had gone? Is that why she had left Fabián? Was it for reasons that had nothing to do with him? Pure coincidence? She remembered how her mother, instead of managing her grief, had started crawling into bed as soon as she got home from work to devote herself to crying: crying loudly, shamelessly, as she stared at the picture of her little sister, dressed in red, wearing the polka dotted shoes she had been gifted the day of the accident. At first Elsa thought she was crying because of her father's death, but later she realized that her grief was much deeper, older, and that nothing could silence it. Her mother was crying out of the grief of being alive, of having outlived her own family, and she no longer thought about Elsa.

They had been a happy family, a happy family like any other, with a father, a mother and two daughters, a nice house in a proper neighborhood, the huge jacaranda tree by the door. Now she was the only one left. Just you, Elsa, just you. Her mother repeated it as if it were her fault, as if Elsa should not go on living, as if she herself, stubborn in her grief, had already died as well.

One day, before leaving for campus, Elsa approached the room where her mother was sleeping and accidentally made the hallway's wood floor creak. Her mother, startled, came out of her narcotic slumber and, seeing Elsa, said simply:

"Oh, I was dreaming and thought you were your sister, but it was just you."

Besides, those were awful years, Elsa reasoned to herself, a time when no one could predict what would happen tomorrow. The emptying of the university, the military coup, the canceled classes, the friends disappeared or leaving. Who, in those years, would have chosen to stay? And the insistence of her mother's lawyer to hand over her inheritance, as if he were advising, without daring to say it outright, that she get out of there.

Below, hovering over the blunt outline of Brazil, the clouds resemble tempera brush strokes. It's a crystal-clear day and, over the American continent, the veins of those tremendous rivers are beating. It's been years since she's seen something so lovely: the kind of immense nature that doesn't exist in Europe, the torpid density of the palm trees, the populations half hidden in the jungle. For a moment she thought of her husband. What must he be doing? A while later the plane started to descend, and the pilot's impersonal voice announced that they would be landing soon.

"Mom, I want to talk to you."

Elsa looked up from studying her plane ticket and knit her brows trying to feign a deep interest; the effort made her go a bit cross-eyed.

"What's the matter, Fabián?"

Fabián. How had she ever agreed to give her son the same name as her first boyfriend? Of course, Elsa had never told her husband anything about the first Fabián's existence. It was a coincidence. Her husband's grandfather and father were also named Fabián, an uncommon name in Spain, and she tepidly protested the proposition to carry on with the tradition:

"But your name isn't Fabián. . ."

"My father's was, and he would have loved it."

It's true, Elsa thought, the old man would have loved it. Her husband's father had just died. He was an astonishing elderly man who, for years now, had zipped around in a wheelchair at full speed; as a young man he had been a cyclist and now, tied to this chair, he seemed to entertain himself. Elsa loved her father-in-law; she liked his humor, rough as a cheese grater, his sharp yet affectionate irony. She wasn't even bothered by his Neolithic ideas, or his house furnished like a notary's office, or his permanent nostalgia for the good old days. The truth was, the old man had welcomed her without prejudice and indulged all of her eccentricities without ever pestering her.

"Look, marrying someone who works in dental prosthetics," he used to say to her, "it's uninteresting, Elsa. How could you not get bored, young lady? I wanted my son to be a bullfighter. And what ever happened to your braid? Missy, you've gone and cut off your pigtail."

Whatever her husband did, he never could have fulfilled the old man's expectations, which, by the way, were constantly changing. I wanted him to be a doctor, an astronaut, a beekeeper. Can you imagine, Elsa, all that free honey? He would say this licking his lips like a cat, as he discreetly spread a forbidden sweet on his toast. Imagine if he had been named Fabián like me. . . It wouldn't be the same for you, being married to a man named Fabián. And he said it with a little smile that made her blood freeze. Damn oracle, damn old man, Elsa would think, stroking his hand. She had never mentioned her first boyfriend in Spain, so this was pure coincidence. And so Elsa agreed to name her son Fabián, but she didn't tell her husband that it was also the name of the person she had loved most in the world. And there her love had stayed, along with Fabián's name, in that heavy and ominous, "Mom, I want to talk to you," and her escape to Buenos Aires, before her son could crush her under the weight of his confidences.

Graciela soon tired of her green dress. There was hardly anyone in the city over summer break, and her fantasy of running into Fabián had faded a while ago. All the same, she went into a bar where people were dancing and tried to let herself be carried away by the music.

At first it was just a timid movement. After a few glasses of liquor, she started to lose her footing. The person dancing wasn't her, she thought, it wasn't Graciela, the proper third-year journalism student, the responsible daughter of a responsibly boring family. No, it wasn't her, whose only unique quality was having red hair; there was something tribal about that swaying together as a group, one giant body full of waving arms and legs. And all those mouths, in unison, singing the chorus: *all you need is love, tarararará.*

Outside, in the deserted city, the atavistic tone of the bass barely reverberated, and no one could imagine what was happening: not the neighbors, not her parents, not the professors, not the soldiers who had taken over the city, not the pharmacist on the corner, no one knew anything, she didn't know anything either, her head empty, *all you need is love*, and Fabián's soft touch on her hand that afternoon. Her hand, her hand, her hand. I'm drunk. We're a tribe performing the fertility dance. She liked the idea because it emptied her head of preconceptions; she began shaking her hips. Everything was so easy, so nice. Almost outside of herself, the sweat running down her chest and back, she felt like she could see herself leaving her body, thanks to the alcohol or dancing. As a young girl she had wanted to be a dancer, and now dancing was the only thing that relaxed her. Dancing and dancing, her belly moving in circles, her hips freed, dancing as if it were the last thing she would do in life, the virgin surrendering herself to dance before giving herself to a man. Yes, all you need is love or, better yet: all I need is sex. Giving herself to a man? How old-fashioned. To hell with it all, except for that hand taking her by the waist and crushing her against a fibrous body, those warm lips whispering "red head" so close to her neck. She doesn't see a face, but it doesn't matter. It's not about faces; it's about the beat creeping up her legs towards her pelvis, the man's hips pressed against her own. All the same, Graciela thinks later, if I don't open my eyes, I can imagine I'm doing it with Fabián.

From her childhood, Elsa remembers the Polish bakery, the view of Plaza Irlanda, the stained-glass window, the basement stairs descending into the shadows, and down there her father, the time beater, the laughs, the "don't worry, Elsita, I'll always love you—Mom takes care of your sister and I take care of you—we're so alike that I'll always be by your side, don't worry." And the beater at full speed liquefying time, her sitting behind her father on the bench, like on a motorcycle, him cutting through the air with a persistent *brrrr* like an airplane propeller, her hugging his protective waist, so warm. Then, when she gave him a kiss, the shrouding scent of shaving cream.

The other thing she remembers is that, one afternoon, next to the front door of the house, she found a sparrow. It wasn't a full-grown bird but a chick that had fallen out of its tree, downed no doubt by the wind and the last rain in Buenos Aires. A tiny, disheveled little bird, with feathers like hairs, bulging eyes, glass bones, a yellow and needy beak almost larger than its body, a beak with room for everything: the drops of sugar water, the breadcrumbs, the fly that Elsa caught and made into a purée. The chick didn't live for long, but it was long enough for Elsa to show it to her little sister and tell her, very slowly, so that Mom wouldn't hear:

"I love him more than anything in the whole world."

The girl stared at her with penetrating, bird-like eyes. Then, in the loudest tone she could muster, she launched into a pitiful cry that guillotined the afternoon. She had understood perfectly what Elsa was trying to tell her. Their mother, furious, gave Elsa the only slap of her life, leaving her cheek throbbing; I can't believe it, such a big girl messing with her little sister, you can't be trusted.

You'll pay for this, Elsa thought as she stroked her cheek, you'll pay.

The memory cuts off there. She's unable to recall the day of the accident, the ambulance, the funeral, or the changing layout of the furniture in her sister's room that, little by little, became her own.

Graciela learned from Fabián that he and Elsa had broken up, and she also learned that Elsa had gone to live in Spain and was not coming back.

"We're hardly in touch," Fabián told her one evening when they met up at the student bar, and that same night they made plans to go to the movies.

By way of confidences, they began to meet up on the weekends. If she wanted to see him, Graciela had to endure the test of listening to him talk about Elsa, describing the minutiae of their life as a couple, even seeing him cry. Sometimes she felt like she was spying through a peephole on a scene that attracted and repulsed her at the same time. Sometimes she was, quite simply, carried away by compassion. It hurt, feeling that he was falling in love with her through his memories, that it was in fact Elsa's absence that was bringing them closer. He loved her now because he loved the words that came out of her own mouth, the memory they were able to sketch, the images they evoked, and that love—ghostly and deferred—would bring them together little by little.

It wasn't easy, she thinks now, after so many years with Fabián. She remembers how, soon after they started dating, she got pregnant. Fabián didn't want to have that child, and she acquiesced. She remembers the silences and reservations; she remembers all the times he accidentally called her Elsa; finally, she remembers the humiliation of knowing that she was the second choice, the one he loved less, the woman by his side through the process of elimination.

What is true, after a lifetime together, she asks herself now. Dreams or daily life? Fantasy or fact? She's peeling green apples to make a tart, cutting them in pale crescents; she likes the arid and sugary feel, the crumbly consistency like pressed sand. Fabián loves this tart, and since she retired, she likes to wait for him with food on the table. He should retire too, Graciela thinks, he should retire so we can enjoy the years he has left. And when she says, "the years he has left," she realizes how afraid she is of Fabián dying; since the attack that miraculously left him unharmed, she has nightmares where she sees him in a coffin. Practically without noticing, she's left behind her plans, those turbulent years; it's curious how much this conventional life appeals to her. It doesn't even hurt anymore that she never had children; she just wants to live with Fabián, remain bound to him by that patient love. She dusts the fruit with cinnamon, and the scent invades the kitchen. Spring in Buenos Aires: sticky heat, sudden downpours, fragrant plants. The neighborhood gets so beautiful this time of year. She looks at her reflection in the window and combs through her hair with her fingers. Her hair, once so red, is now the color of pale fruit. She likes it. She's not bothered by the first signs of old age—she's much happier now, she thinks, as the smell of burnt sugar emerges from the oven. She takes off her apron and peers out the window, hoping to see Fabián turning the corner and waving to her with one hand, like he always does.

In the air, far off in the distance, a red balloon floats and sways, like a dot of blood.

When her father found her trying to fit into her little sister's red polka-dotted shoes, he didn't say a word, not even when he saw that the stitching on the heels had given way in her effort to put them on. He stroked her head almost in pity, then took her by the hand and brought her to the basement; tilting his head he studied her in silence, then at last he gifted her the time machine.

"If ever you need me, you know what to do; just turn the crank, and I'll come find you. I'll come out of the black hole."

Elsa hid the gadget among her clothes, and when her father died, she tried to make it work, beating the hours to bring him back, turning and turning the crank until her hands hurt; she returned to the basement and sat alone on the bench in the still darkness, recovering the scent of shaving cream. But that was all. Much later she understood that her father knew he was sick and that he would have to leave her; this childish game was his way of asking her forgiveness for such a fragile life. Finally, Elsa lost the beater during some move and shelved that memory of death, along with so many others.

That's why it's so strange that the poem is coming back to me, she thinks, that's why it's so odd that I got this house.

"It was the flowering season of the year." Peering out from the balcony, as she studies the plaza's gravel paths, the swing sets and the little tables where old folks play dominoes, she feels that she has made the right choice in returning. The house, her old house, is now divided into various apartments to be rented out to tourists; the stained-glass windows have been broken and then replaced, mostly by other, colorless ones; the door leading to the basement is blocked off. The study, her parents' bedroom and the big bathroom have also ended up on the other side of the wall. This makes her a bit melancholy, but at the same time it seems easier to contain: the house was too big, she tells herself, too full of secrets. The balcony is the same, and the jacaranda tree, ever taller, is bursting with violet buds. Fabián, Fabián, Fabián. She's dreamed of him too much recently and they were sensual dreams; she wrote to him at his workplace, and he responded with a glowing letter saying that he would love to see her: "I'd love to see you, Elsa, and hear what's happened in all this time—we have a lot to discuss." Then she gathered the courage to call him at work and they began speaking giddily, talking over each other like teenagers. And, finally, they decided to meet today. Yes, to bring their chapters to a close and write an epilogue, just the two of them. How tempting it is to go back and pick up the story where they left off. They settled on meeting there, at her house: it's discreet. Soon she'll see him approach and ring the doorbell, like when they were young.

The girl runs after the pigeon. This morning she managed to get her mother to dress her in her dance shoes, the red polka-dotted shoes that she adores and that are not for playing in the park. She also managed to get the little dress and the red stockings, and finally, the most important thing: for her sister to look at her with envy. What's more, her sister has to keep an eye on her, which makes her the girl's slave. Their mother is in the kitchen and shouts:

"Elsa, watch your little sister from the window, she's going down to the plaza! Don't let her out of your sight—OK, Elsa? You heard me?"

Elsa hid the box with the sparrow under her bed; if her mother finds it, she'll tell her to throw out that nasty vermin immediately. Her mother hates birds: they have evil little eyes, she says. Evil little eyes.

She peers out over the balcony and watches her sister run over the gravel paths, cut through the area where the old people are playing dominoes, her red balloon appearing and disappearing among the treetops. She's sick and tired of keeping an eye on that little flea. She hates her. Ever since she was born, everything has been about her: Elsa, look at your little sister, Elsa, feed her, Elsa, make her bed, Elsa,

Elsa! Her sister moves out of her field of vision, and Elsa, bored, leaves the window for a moment to look at the hatchling. She's about to return to her watch post when suddenly she thinks, fuck her. And she basks in the word: fuck-her. She and her stupid polka-dotted shoes. Her mother can also go fuck herself. Let her watch over the girl. The chick is barely moving; maybe the fly was bad for him, maybe he needs more water. He's gasping with his ugly yellow beak, not opening his eyes; his eyelids are pallid membranes. Poor sparrow, Elsa thinks, she'll have to find somewhere to bury him. She hears brakes slamming, screams. Outside, on the street, a car's blood-stained tracks, people running and forming a crowd, and in the center of the chaos, the polka-dotted shoes in a strange position. She raises her gaze to the sky and sees the red balloon floating, swaying in the air.

The time beater, her father's machine, she, a child, clinging to his waist, pressing against his back. Where did she put it? It would do her good to have it now, she thinks, as she waits for Fabián. Things have gone resoundingly well. She traveled alone, everything is going according to plan. Now the carefully made bed. The morning at the hair salon. The perfume. That same perfume Fabián used to like. She could tell him that she named her son after him, and as she's thinking about it, she fantasizes that they could have had that son together. She could tell him so many things, a mixture of truths and fibs. For instance, that she's tired of being married to a dental prosthetist, that they could be lovers. Lovers. Why not? She savors the word. No theatrics, no drama. They don't even need to air their passion. Why would they, at this point? Why hurt anyone? It's about accepting what's there: two realities, two worlds, two loves, two seasons, two countries. Perfect. This story would have amused her father-in-law. She imagines telling it to him, erasing the rim of guilt that she still feels. What nonsense. Elsa smiles thinking about this autumnal love that's out of a movie, the little lies she'll have to concoct, the shame of undressing, the slow and shy sex, dimly lit of course, the nice wines they can drink together in bed as they listen to the Beatles, for example, and reminisce about their college years, or read poems by Dylan Thomas. And Góngora, the ever-present Góngora with his flowering season. Old age is the flowering season, she thinks, the moment when everything comes together and is fulfilled, even the most dejected dreams. For the first time in years, she feels hopeful, young, above all happy.

The man sitting on the park bench has a date with his first girlfriend and is waiting for the time to come. He's quite anxious and should call home and invent some sort of excuse, although he knows that his wife won't put up a fuss; she never does, at most the food will get cold, and she will forgive him. His wife always understands, it's the best thing about her, yet also the most tiresome: there's something dull about women who always understand. He feels a jab of guilt and pushes the thought away, this is not the time to be thinking about her. He's agreed to see Elsa with genuine desire, with haste, and also with fear, because this life that he has today, this fragile, cracked life, could break down through its own fissures. He breathes, worked up, then relaxes. Today is about living, about enjoying the present. It's a precious morning in early spring; the buds on the trees are a stirring pale green, the tree trunks seem darker and the pigeons coo chasing after one another, flying towards a little old woman who tosses them bread. Because of his nerves, he got there early. He needs to calm down, he doesn't want her to notice. He's dressed in smart casual, just like he used to wear back then; deep down nothing has changed that much. He hasn't even lost his hair, he tells himself with pride; although he has gray hairs they suit him; he stays slim, and he's positive that his eyes are handsome. What will it be like to start all over again? He likes rites: he was the one who was dumped, so she's the one who has to win him back. She's the one who left, so it has to be her coming back to him. What pleasure it gives him to be in her hands. In fact, she was the one who looked him up. He received a letter, then a call at work with an altered name that made him feel resoundingly young. She has the same voice, that slightly childish voice that he loves. What if he doesn't recognize her? Of course he will, she can't have changed that much. All morning he's felt a bit dizzy, and now he's trying to relax, calm himself down. He loosens the knot on his tie. He feels a sudden pain and, as he falls, he touches his chest. It's humiliating to crawl, his pants stained with dirt; he's so hunched over that he can't cry out, unable to reach his pills. It's his second attack, he knows it will be the end if no one helps him. At eye level, he sees two polka-dotted shoes, like the ones flamenco dancers wear, red stockings, and the rolling hem of a little red dress. A girl holding a balloon approaches and studies him; suddenly she turns and starts chasing a pigeon; she runs after the birds that, at her abrupt movement, take flight. The girl throws herself after them and lets go of the balloon, which is the last thing the man sees, swaying in the air, before he closes his eyes, before the breaks slam, before the crash sounds, before the sirens start to wail.

Writing

For Javier Sáez de Ibarra, because of a chat over coffee

THE PRESSURE cooker is just starting to hiss when there's a knock at the door. I open and a young woman with Asian features appears; without a word she sits down in my kitchen. The chickpeas are fragrant; the twins must be leaving school now. As I'm trying to arrange my schedule, I release the pressure from the pot, and the kitchen fills with a shot of steam that startles Lyuba. Because the girl is named Lyuba—I know it, though not all characters' names are so clear. Lyuba approaches the pot with caution, and I understand that in her world pressure cookers do not exist. When I serve up the chickpeas she starts devouring them with her hands, like a little animal: curious teeth, thin hands, breasts like two olives. Tonight, after class, I have to present a friend's novel; I run through the talk in my head. My daughters arrive with their comforting, quotidian hustle and bustle, wanting to tell me something as a duet; luckily Lyuba exists only for me and seems discreet. I remember the time I lived with a suicidal man who dragged around the rope he used to hang himself. And the Russian nobleman, who reeked of seal, or that Nazi soldier, who searched for victims even inside of the washing machine. Now it's Lyuba, just Lyuba. As I'm pretending to listen, I feel the need to write, and the urge makes me feel guilty. The girls start fighting in stereophony. Lyuba studies them, breaking into a smile that falls somewhere between scathing and flirtatious. She takes advantage of the twins getting up from the table, leans closer and whispers: "My father raped me." The sentence echoes like a bomb. She sits back down, as if the information had to do with something like the weather forecast. She could have said, "I'm looking for a boyfriend" or "I don't know what to study" or "I want to go bungee jumping"; this confidence is the starting gun for a tremendous story. I bring the twins to the sports center. I should stop at the salon, although if I just put my hair up, I'll look fine and I'll have more of the afternoon to write. I also have to go visit my father, who's sick. What surprises me about Lyuba's confiding is not the story about her father, but rather the fact that she spoke to me in French. Lyuba is a Nenet, one of those nomadic people who live near the Arctic, whose language I'm unfamiliar with. I search on the internet and find their customs: reindeer herding, tents with a central stove, fur garments. They're sitting on the largest gas reserves on the planet, which is why the Russians are trying to decimate them. I remember reading a novel about Eskimos. What was it called? *Top of the World.* Yes. I should reread it. I find a series of ethnographic facts that don't interest me. What a misfortune it is to live on top of a treasure chest, I think. I jot down the idea so as not to forget. "The misfortune of good." I like it for a while, then I lose interest—it's stupid, Truman Capote already developed that idea in *Answered Prayers.* Wikipedia: "Over the winter, the Nenets travel to the Polar Circle to look for lichens for their reindeer." My head hurts; I call my mother, who says my father is not doing well. I go back to the kitchen. Lyuba is still there, and now I can study her. She's odd, but very beautiful. Black hair down her back, long neck, powerful limbs. She opens her legs. She's not wearing underwear, and I see the brush of her sex, which smells like lichens. She waits to see how I react, but I don't fall for her provocation, I simply stand in front of her; now she's closed her knees and is staring at me defenselessly. I shut myself in my study, write. And erase. How old must Lyuba be? It's hard for me to tell how old Asian-looking people are. I wonder if that comment was racist. I need to research the emotions of girls who have been raped. Phone: they try to sell me something or other, a woman talks but I don't understand her—maybe she has French heritage, or Eskimo. I must have answered brusquely because she hangs up in a huff. My mother again, now she seems very nervous. I tell her no, there's not a chance I can come tonight, early tomorrow morning for sure. I feel the urge to talk to my friend Pilar, who just adopted an Eskimo girl, but I leave that for later; besides, she might be bothered by my prying. I run to pick up the twins from the sports center, I'll stop by the store on the way. And what about the salon? With the rest of the chick-peas, I can make a hummus for my in-laws—it always comes out great. Luckily the twins are girls; if they had been boys, one of them would have had to been named after my father-in-law, Fermín. I love my father-in-law dearly, sometimes I think I married his son to be closer to him. What nonsense. And what to do about my father? Put on makeup: there will be press at the book talk, and I look like a vampire. The sun is setting, it's cold. As I drive down the highway, I think that the best thing that could happen would be for me to end up in the middle of a traffic jam, alone for hours, but traffic flows in the gray evening. The twins are exhausted. I give up on going to the hair salon and the store. I just need to drop them off at home, get my books, change for the presentation, teach my class. I send a quick message to my husband, asking him to make dinner. He sends me a loving text, to which I don't reply. I feel guilty again. When I leave the twins in the parking lot, Lyuba is there waiting for me with a huge suit-case; she pushes it into the car, and we don't talk during the ride—I'm able to focus on preparing my class. All of a sud-den, in a monotonous little voice, she tells me a story of cold and abuse. She speaks of a mammoth hidden in the ice, she says that she was adopted, that she wants to travel. She says that she's found something in Normandy. In Normandy?, I ask her, puzzled. Yes, she says, and starts talking without restraint. My head is exploding. If I had any sense, I would stop on the next corner and push Lyuba out of the car. I would leave her in the middle of some road; I would, at the very least, ask her to stop talking. But I don't do it; her rambling story fascinates me. Shit, I'm late and I've left my notes at home. Lyuba sits at the back of the classroom. I appreciate her courtesy and silence, and I fondly muse that she should find someone who truly loves her: a family, a boyfriend. I wish her lovely afternoons lying in the sun, on some beach in Normandy. I outline a few premises, but they all seem terribly sappy: I strike through what I've written in my notebook. I get to the presentation late; the photographers are already feasting on the author. I say my four sentences with little enthusiasm; really, I did the bare minimum whereas I had wanted to be much more emphatic. What's more, I look hideous. I drink a Coke. Lyuba, on the other hand, seems to have drunk all the alcohol reserves for the night and is laughing like a buccaneer; she seems determined to flirt with anyone who crosses her path. I drag her stumbling out of the reception, and push her, swaying, into a taxi as she insults everyone who passes by. She takes a strange coin out of her pocket, shows it to me as if it were a treasure; it's a dollar with a hole—one of those ones that people hang around their necks—then she throws it out the window. The coin rebounds, shining in the middle of the night, and a very handsome young man with tattoos all over his body picks it up. He looks German and smiles at Lyuba, who tries to get out of the car, but luckily I'm able to stop her. Finally we rush off; she settles down on the drive, and by the time we arrive home she's calmer. I clean her face as if she were a child and tuck her into bed. She's naked, her slender body so beautiful that it makes me shiver. Lyuba doesn't seem to be aware of herself, she's growing weak, I cover her with a duvet, tell her to relax, everything will be alright; I lie down next to her, giving her my heat. Then she examines me with those little marble eyes, stretches out her arms, where the marks of her father's violence show through, breathes like a frightened animal, places my hand on her nipples and, though I try to let go, she holds me down with her stubborn strength—I sense her snowy stench as she drives her sharp little teeth into my throat. Resigned, I outstretch my neck. The house is quiet: everyone is sleeping. I write.

Albania

For Julieta

"EVERYONE NEEDS an enemy, an enemy to keep you awake."

The sentence sprang into the mind of the young man who, half asleep and outstretched on the seat of the train, clutches his backpack. People have warned him about Albanians climbing onto trains and robbing passengers; all sorts of tales travel the tracks. He shivers a little, comes out of his nightmare, looks out the window and sees the sign: Angoulême—finally, he's in France.

It's summer, early morning. In the deserted station, the switchman signals for a luxury sleeper train to enter. A red-haired woman looks out the window: oversized t-shirt, nails painted gumdrop red. She stretches and becomes aware of the young man watching her; at first she covers her shoulders, but then, with a provocative smile, she stares back, parts her lips and presses her breasts against the glass. Although it looks like a game, the young man blushes; he's never been with a woman before, and this one is almost too good-looking. He also leans against the glass, but in that very moment, the train starts moving. Before the young man disappears, the red-haired woman raises the palm of her hand, as if wanting to caress him.

It's ten to seven in the morning, and the only person left in the station is an old man who's sitting on a wooden bench petting a dog. The red-haired woman covers her shoulders again; she's about to return to her bunk when she hears her husband snore. It's her honeymoon, and her husband is sleeping. She has known for days now that it was a mistake to get married—they don't have anything in common. Now, for instance, it would have been fun to switch trains, start an affair with the boy. She looks over at the old man who, in turn, studies her, and at the dog, who's dragging his shriveled leg across the platform. Where must the boy be now? He took off going north; they're going to Venice, her husband has booked another expensive hotel: expensive hotels, luxury clothes, designer food and insipid banter. Until death do us part. She leans out onto the platform. Under her sneakers, the tracks are trails of silver. It smells like something burning—oil, iron, the enticing scent of travel. The switchman waves a flag; the doors are about to close. Without thinking, Kristina grabs her luggage, throws it and leaps into the void. Before the train disappears, before her husband discovers her absence, she buys a ticket for a regional train, goes back to looking out another window; amid snarls and groans the train starts moving, the dog runs to catch up to her, the girl leans out, and with a pompous gesture, waves farewell with a hand that cuts through the air.

A little later, she gets off at a random station and decides to hitchhike. It's hard to say no to a red-head; one guy bites instantly and unlocks the door to his Alfa Romeo. Not bad, although he looks a bit like her husband: bougie clothes, bougie car, bougie luggage; there's an exchange of friendly signals that lowers her anxiety. She accepts a cigarette and allows him to use a gold lighter engraved with the initials: C.M. Carlo Macri? Cosimo Mirandolini? The only thing they have in common is that she needs a car and he has one, that she is escaping from a husband and he, according to what he's told her, is going to meet his wife.

Carlo, Cosimo, or whatever the hell his name is, only uses the pronoun "I." Kristina relaxes; it's exhausting to be nice for so long, in a few minutes she's asleep. When she wakes up, they're parking.

"Genoa?"

"It was impossible to wake you in Genoa—my trip ends here."

Then he takes her by the chin and stares into her eyes:

"You'll like Rapallo, go on now, I have to go meet my wife. Do you need money?"—and he places his hand on her thigh.

Kristina looks at the hand like it's a spider; he's a bit taken aback but shrugs his shoulders, picking up his cell phone.

Despite the bad start, Rapallo turns out to be a charming city. She goes on a walk by the bay and ends up getting lost in the winding, narrow streets, where buildings seem to join together before reaching the sky. She sits in a piazza and has a coffee; the marble sidewalks emanate a pleasant cool. Finally she walks through the fishermen's quarter, where she finds a little hotel by the sea.

She wakes up late; as she's going to put on her jeans, she discovers that the man has taken off with her things. She's an idiot. How could she not realize? She doesn't have anything to wear; besides, her husband may have canceled her cards by now. If so, she'll have to stay dressed like this for the rest of her life in order to purge her sins. In a store she chooses something at random, holds out her card and a cheerful tune authorizes it: wave of gratitude. If things don't work out, she can still call him. Yes, she could call him right now, but she's feeling fragile, not ready to deal with fits of rage. Instead, she writes: "I'm OK. Please forgive me, if you can."

As she's strolling along, she finds some sandals, a pair of pants with a certain flair, a spacious orange handbag that she falls in love with, a huge black silk scarf. She distracts herself by remembering the train, the pallid morning, her husband's snores, the boy's face watching her from the window. It's just a vacation: she has cash, credit cards, free time, she's young. Why not carry on by herself? She goes up to the room to gather her few belongings. Opening the guidebook to a random page and closing her eyes, she lets her finger drop on the map: Ancona.

She studies herself in a store window: is that her? The woman looking at herself in the reflection? The one who, without recourse, is approaching thirty? She walks into a hair salon.

"Wash and cut. Very short."

"Sure you won't regret it?"

She leaves stroking the needles of hair. Then, in the station, she repeats:

"Ancona."

She likes the fact that it begins with "A." She tries to pay with her card but the employee, after swiping it several times, hands it back to her; it might be the card reader, he says, don't worry, nothing works around here. She pays in cash and sits down to wait. It's summer, why stress, everyone is dawdling about, when she's finished she'll go back to France and look for work, as an interpreter, a flight attendant. Good idea: speaking different languages and meeting new people. She could find a job, a man she likes, start a family, take out a loan, buy a house, get a dog.

"What a scary thought."

She's about to call her husband to tell him what's going on; she has to face him sometime, if not now, when, although maybe it would be better to call him tomorrow—yes, for sure. She asks if there's somewhere to sit in the café, and the waiter points to a corner of the bar.

"Over there, next to the Albanian woman."

Against the tiled wall there's a woman trying to organize her parcels; the high ceiling dwarfs her. She clutches her handbag. With her hand hidden like a mouse she counts her money, takes out an envelope, studies some papers, rereads them moving her lips, then looks at Kristina, as if asking for her approval. Why is she smiling at her? Maybe for fun, maybe she thinks that Kristina, with her black scarf and her orange handbag, is just like her—a migrant. Feeling uneasy, she steps out onto the platform. Summer, she says to herself: the word is her talisman. Over the darkened city, the sky is turquoise.

On the train she gets cold and covers herself with the silk scarf, which immediately starts to float like a black cloud. Whether or not her card works, she'll look for a hotel by the sea.

Sitting next to her is a young, tattooed man who smiles at her. He's very tall and blond; seeing his muscled body, she's tempted to strike up a conversation. But better not; men have only complicated her life lately.

Little by little the city slips away as they advance through a mountainous landscape. Little lighted cottages that look like toys. Looking at the gardens, she's surprised by her hunger for domestic life. A little boy runs down the aisle. Would she like to have children someday? Encircled by mountains, the train slows down. The mother looks at her with a question in her eyes, then calls her son. Someone next to her says:

"I'd love to have a son like that."

It's the tattooed hunk. Kristina smiles at him, and he talks as if he knew her, showing her a picture of his girl-friend and saying that he's going to meet her on the beach, in Normandy. . .

"But you're going south. . ."

"She has exams right now, so I'm waiting for her—traveling and gathering the courage to ask her to marry me."

His sincerity appeals to her: why hasn't she found a man like this, simply in love? She's envious of the girl in the photo, of her luck.

"How do I ask her?"

In the middle of nowhere, the train stops. Passengers peer out onto the track; in the silent night a strong scent of pine wafts. Someone says the train hit something, probably a large animal. Outside lights are streaming, illuminating bursts of green; she hears the ticket collector shouting, two people dressed in white whisper. Soon, a "here, quick!" echoes from behind the glass, a siren pierces the countryside, a dog howls. No one comments when the train starts moving again. Kristina returns to the balm of conversation:

"How do you ask her? I don't know, leave it to chance. . ."

"Good idea," says the guy. "Chance."

"What's your tattoo?"

"It just says *wie alt*, over and over again. Do you like it? It's an homage to my grandmother, she almost died in Mauthausen. . ." And the guy takes out another photograph, of a smiling old woman with big, dark eyes. "She's Spanish, you know? She says what saved her was seeing a tear of compassion in a stranger's eye. Isn't that wild? Just a drop of compassion. Two Spanish grandparents, two Polish grandparents, and I was born in Buenos Aires: I'm a genetic accident."

The guy rattles on with an extremely complicated story about his grandmother and the train, then something about a crying switchman; he mixes some Polish bakers into the story—my grandparents, he says—they're sad stories, and Kristina tunes out; she's tired. A while later, the young man also seems to have lost interest and stares out the window.

The landscape traces a crossbow curve; the wheels screech; they get so close to the water that it seems the sea will flood the cars. It's a summer sea, innocent. She keeps her eyes closed for a few moments; when she opens them everything seems to have returned to normal—the young man with the tattoos is no longer there, and next to the sleeping boy, the mother dozes as well. Surrounded by cliffs, the sea licks the feet of Ancona: everything is water and the huge mass of cruise ships, mastheads, yachts.

She hurries through the station in search of a taxi while avoiding the destitute; an albino puppy trots up to her. She pets him on the head; the warm touch makes her recall, nostalgically, the morning she jumped off the train, the boy, the dog, the old man. It's very late. A few cars slow down when they see the red-haired woman, one taxi stops. The driver looks Arab and doesn't exactly inspire confidence, but he has a picture of his children on the dashboard, which eases her nerves. He turns around to study her:

"Where am I taking you?"

"A nice hotel."

"Let's go to Sirolo, yes, Sirolo. There are people like you there."

"How long will it take?"

"It takes what it takes, no more and no less."

Hugging her orange handbag, she tries to relax. The nape of the driver's neck looks like a bull's, with swirls of coarse hair. Although at first she thought he was Arab, he is, clearly, an Italian from the south.

They leave the city behind, plunging deep into the darkness, beginning to turn in ever-tightening curves; the night is so dense it looks like someone struck through it. Finally, a faded glow peeks through and comes into definition, along with the first buildings, haloed by light, of a mouth-watering village.

"Sirolo," the taxi driver says. "Don't you like it?" and he turns around again to look at her legs. "Oh, I didn't turn on the meter. . . How much should I charge you? Eh, signorina? How much should I charge you?"

Typical: people from the south.

"You know what? I won't charge you for the ride; at the end of the day, it's only brought me closer to home. Look— my wife's down there waiting for me with dinner."

Kristina chooses the most expensive room, has her dress ironed, and goes downstairs to eat dinner in the garden suspended over the cliffs: opulent houses surrounded by trees hang in the darkness. It's late, the hydrangeas are nodding off in terracotta pots, their recently watered leaves shining. She orders an expensive wine, shrimp salad and seafood ravioli in a squid ink sauce. Behind the hydrangeas she sees a trickle of smoke, and connected to it, there's a man smiling at her. He's somewhat older, handsome like an old-fashioned heartthrob, with large, predictable eyes. He leaves before her and nods goodbye. When she goes to pay, the waiter tells her that Mr. Tassi has taken care of the bill and hands her his card. She stays on the terrace smoking as the sea folds and unfolds its monotonous groan. On fresh sheets, she sleeps like never before.

She's awakened by a sun that drops onto her pillow like a gold coin and by someone knocking at the door. The house-keeper enters energetically, and along with the breakfast tray, brings her a note. It's the man from last night proposing that they have dinner together. "On my boat," he says, add-ing, "I'm harmless, I'll be a good host, everybody knows me."

She does some research around the hotel, and everyone speaks highly of Tassi. He's the son of the owner of Dórico Shoes, does business in construction, stocks, and who knows what else—an old-money Ancona family. She takes a walk in the woods, getting lost on the dirt paths, enjoying the deep green of the trees that let the sea peek through. She goes down to Ancona to buy clothes, and the city also seems nice. She finds some gold sandals, a very low-cut dress that noth-ing in the world can stop her from showing off tonight.

She spends the afternoon in a miraculously empty cove where she swims naked, her hair like a dash of saffron. She lies down, rests, dozing off at times. Curiously, she recalls the young man she saw a thousand years ago, in Angoulême, imagining him there, next to her.

"Mr. Tassi," a secretary's voice announced, "Mr. Leonardo Tassi says a taxi will come pick you up at eight."

She looked at herself in the mirror: the sandals weren't too comfortable, but they made for a magnificent look: tight-fitting dress, breasts served on a platter, nude back trailing down to her tailbone. She took her scarf. Before eight she was at the hotel door, and the same taxi that brought her to Sirolo was arriving.

"Signore Tassi asked me to treat you like a treasure, he said, in those same words. You'll see what kind of boat. . ."

The Dórico was an arrogant yacht that reflected hundreds of colored glimmers onto the water; she had to give her name and wait as the person in charge of security looked her up on the list. At the top of the stairs, smoking in between coughs, stood a homely young woman who was already considerably drunk. She stumbled down the stairs—Kristina almost had to grab her—but instead of saying thanks, she pulled her arm away, rubbing it as though she had been stung by a wasp. Then she lifted her dress up to her waist and dropped onto the dock with her legs crossed. From there she threw an innocent smile into the air and studied Kristina.

"Nice sandals, very nice, better than the ones my father makes."

And she murmured:

"I'm warning you, everything here is in very bad taste. Even my name. Look at our yacht—it's named after a shoe manufacturer!"

She stood up, stumbling, and with an almost comic solemnity held out her hand:

"I'm Mimi Tassi, a reader by trade, a rich man's daughter and, from this night on, a drunkard. Only liquor, not like those people up there, who'd snort the olives if they could."

"Mimi!", shouted a voice with a foreign accent. "What are you doing on the dock? Come back right now!"

"That's my father's ex. Hey, Cleavage, nice dress."

Immersed in the set of an old movie, Tassi was waiting for her at the top of the stairs. Kristina let him kiss her hand and introduce her to a series of older men who hungrily gazed at her; she allowed kisses stabbed like pins from a series of women who must have shared a bed with Mr. Tassi; she let her glass be filled so many times that, an hour later, she couldn't hold herself up on her sandals. It was almost daybreak when the guests, like dragonflies, began to dissipate. Then Mr. Tassi caught her by the waist.

"You're staying, right?"

Though he addressed her informally, it made no difference; she found it impossible to abandon the "sir" that the man seemed to have etched on his forehead. And how could she tell him no—the sandals were killing her—besides, with the amount of alcohol in her veins she couldn't possibly go anywhere. It was almost day when she saw her sandals again, floating around Mr. Tassi's tanned torso. With a mastery worthy of applause, Mr. Tassi had made love to her: every pore, every fold, every bud, a long-practiced ceremony. Then they had shared a cigarette while staring at the designs on the ceiling. And, by the time the sun emerged over the sea, they had fallen asleep, turned back to back.

"Cleavage! What are you doing wrapped in a sheet? Everyone's outside. Are you coming for breakfast? You don't have clothes? Girl, don't worry—if there's one thing there's too much of on this boat it's women's clothes."

Mimi's little face peeks through the porthole. But instead of the Mimi from last night, it's a near child stripped of her ugliness and nonsense. Her hair is dripping with water and she's wearing a bathing suit that looks old. She hugs herself, goosebumps covering her skin.

"I've decided to turn over a new leaf: I don't drink anymore. By the way, Cleavage, nice ass, it looks real. Dad's ex had hers done. . . They've replaced her piece by piece; I don't think she exists anymore."

She says it with the tone of an experienced woman, then immediately bites her nails.

"Come on, Mimi, be good, I'm dying for a coffee, I want to leave."

"We won't get there until tonight, and that's if Dad doesn't decide to stop here and there to show off his motorboat. Have you seen the motorboat? Coffee or a martini?

"Tell your father to call me a taxi . . ."

"We set sail hours ago, I thought you knew Dad."

"I didn't bring anything. . ."

"They'll never control us. Corfu is a pain in the ass, but it's divine—we can go shopping. If you promise to go with me, I'll bring you coffee. Think it over, Cleavage, it's not a bad deal: alone on this boat you're lost."

On the deck, caressed by a pleasant breeze, there were various couples taking in the sun; Tassi chatted animatedly with a woman as sinuous as Roger Rabbit's girlfriend. Every once in a while, he would kiss her on her lips and she would let him do it, making the face of someone who doesn't want her makeup ruined. Martinis were distributed and everyone seemed absorbed in the thrilling task of fishing for olives in their glasses.

When Mr. Tassi saw her, he put on a toothy grin.

"How did you sleep? Did Mimi bother you? Have you seen what a nice day it is? Do you want something to drink?"

As they touched cheeks, brunette Jessica Rabbit inspected her tits, seemed to recognize her disadvantage, and turned her back again. The few who had survived the party did not seem to be in good shape, and behind their dark glasses, they passed through the deck; Mr. Tassi went out to debut his motorboat, but he didn't invite her to come, so she stayed behind alone with "everyone." They were eating salads, canapés and watermelon soaked in alcohol, tons of alcohol.

The rest of the afternoon passed monotonously, just like the sea. Outside of the bedroom, Tassi turned out to be viscerally dull, and Mimi was reading a very long book. When she tried to approach, the girl threw her a haughty look that made her stiffen. Then she seemed to feel bad.

"Come on, Cleavage, be good, go entertain yourself for a bit."

"I won't go shopping with you. . ."

"And what, you're going to spend a week in that dress? Think about the gold sandals for a minute. . . Be a good girl— let me finish this chapter and then I'll take care of you."

It was almost night when they reached Corfu. In the port, parked between huge yachts, shined the headlights of a car that brought them to a mansion in a rustic part of the island. Kristina decided to have a good time, and so when they sat down for dinner on the terrace, she was nice to the rest of the guests; later they migrated to the armchairs to leaf through magazines. Mimi was sprawled on a sofa reading. Aside from brunette Jessica Rabbit, who stayed on the terrace supported by her glass, the rest evaporated, tossing kisses into the air—Mr. Tassi was also swallowed up by the carpeted hallway. From the terrace, the brunette studied him amusedly; it was becoming clear that she knew much more about Tassi than Kristina would have liked to admit, and, shaking her dark mane, she approached the balustrade, looked at the mainland to be discerned on the other shore, and murmured:

"*Alvaní kakí. . .*"

Mimi closed her book and raised her eyes in infinite disdain. Then she went over and sat next to Kristina:

"She's always going on about the same thing; what do we care."

"What's she saying?"

"Can't you see? Look, right in front of us—those mountains and that light, a bay far more beautiful than all of this: the Ionian, Cleavage. The Ionian, the sea of Odysseus, Nausicaa, the land of the Phaeacians." Then she studied her and lowered her voice:

"I see, you have no idea what I'm talking about. What's going on in that head of yours, other than that pretty red hair? Oh well, keep the travel brochure: pebble beaches, snow-capped mountains—even in the summer. That's what bothers the Greeks."

"Your stepmother's Greek?"

"No and yes. That is, no she's not my stepmother, unless my father marries her again, which he does every once in a while. And yes, she's Greek. We bought this house for her; she's always led my father around by the nose."

Kristina peered out over the terrace and saw the lights. It had been such a crazy trip that she didn't even know where she was; Corfu sounded like somewhere people would "summer," like Empress Sissi, like "luxury island getaways" in Greece or Italy. In the sapphire blue night, the moon's perfect circle shone. Out in the distance, the last light's glow traced a silhouette of the coast.

"Albania," Mimi said, and tucked her little hand into Kristina's, got up on her tiptoes, and whispered in her ear: "That moron, every time she sees this gem, says the same thing: 'evil Albanians.' Tomorrow, before they wake up, we'll cross over to Saranda. You promised, Cleavage, you promised. There's nothing interesting to buy here in Corfu. Tomorrow we'll be eating breakfast in Albania."

It was very early when Mimi appeared in her room.

"I'm trying to look older. Here, put this on. I couldn't find any shoes—you're screwed—you'll have to make do with the sandals. Look at this cool hat."

"Leave it, I'll wear my scarf."

"For whatever we fancy," she said, taking out a fistful of bills. "OK, now show me how to put on makeup."

A little while later, as they chatted away on the ferry, they saw emerge, amid hundreds of orange and olive trees, the coast of Albania.

Saranda is a gorgeous city, located on a large bay with an ample view of the villages perched on the mountains. It used to be a pirate stronghold; now it's a peaceful setting where, in summer, the Greeks outnumber the Albanians. It looks like Europe forty years ago, when nature was authentic and not everything looked like an amusement park. Men walked arm in arm, followed by chattering women. Kristina, expecting something more exotic, found them not unlike the residents of any other southern place.

They ate breakfast watching cruise ships and ocean liners pass by; every once in a while, an Italian speedboat would patrol the coast to prevent the traffic of illegal migrants. A bit uneasy, Kristina remembered that she didn't have any form of identification, or any money, but what did it matter as long as she was with the girl. Sitting by her side, Mimi studied her in bliss.

It was mid-morning, and tourists were drinking in the sun. One woman laid a cloth on the ground and spread out embroidered tablecloths. More than fat she was sturdy, with short legs, wide hips. Her face was covered by a scarf that framed her smile, which widened when she approached to peddle something. She spoke a hodgepodge of languages that always shared some similar word, and her eagerness to sell the tablecloths resulted in valiant attempts to communicate. Kristina liked her enthusiasm, the energy she spent on her work; it struck her that, soon, maybe she too would have to sharpen her wits in order to survive. Mimi's high-pitched voice broke her out of her trance:

"So annoying," she said loudly, making a crude hand gesture.

Kristina startled. The woman had taken out a bag of oranges and was now offering them to the girls. Seeing as she had nothing to pay her with, she tried to send the woman away with a smile, but Mimi cut through the exchange with another blunt phrase that made the Albanian woman jump back. She held the oranges tight against her chest, spat on the ground and turned to another table.

"What did you say to her, Mimi?"

"Look, Cleavage, I'm not an NGO; I hate these gypsies, if you get distracted they'll rob you," and she gripped her bag with an ostentatious distrust. We came here to have a good time. By the way, you could put in a bit more effort with my father: wouldn't you like to become my stepmother?"

As if she had said something too intimate, she changed the topic, hiding behind her wise monkey mask:

"Shall we go to Butrint? It has temples, theatres, it's like Greece. . . Not everything is about shopping and more shopping, you know—we'll deal with your shoes later."

A strong orange smell rose up behind them. With a grim look on their faces, two young men were chewing the fruit; the older one, strong and olive-toned, was playing with a pocketknife; the other one had a violin and started playing in an irritating way—it seemed like a signal. Instantly, a man appeared, dressed like a peasant; he sat down next to the woman, and they whispered, pointing indiscreetly at the girls; then he took out a bottle and started drinking from the neck. Kristina sensed that the environment was becoming oppressive and stood up on the heels that were already starting to bother her, tugging the girl.

"Let's go."

As they walked away, she sensed that the sound of the violin was getting closer and closer.

Kristina was already completely fed up with walking by the time they arrived in Butrint, not so much because of Mimi, who was walking beside her and explaining every ruin they encountered, but more so because the sandals were destroying her feet.

"We'll go shopping later—you're stepping on Byzantine mosaics, Cleavage, everything is Venetian, or Roman, or Greek. Let's go see the lagoon, it's amazing, we can take a taxi if you want. And don't complain so much, we'll go right back to Saranda after.

She had imagined Albania as a barren land, but the lush nature around Butrint accompanied them every step of the way. Finally, when the light began to fade, Kristina stood her ground:

"Mimi, these heels are killing me."

She wasn't just exhausted but also furious at her own foolishness. She was dependent on this girl, who swung between reasonable conversation and the volatile attacks of a rich kid. Why had she let herself be dragged to Albania? Now Mimi was watching her with contempt.

By means of sitting down and refusing to walk, she managed to get them on one of the last return trips to Saranda; when they arrived, the bars were practically deserted and the businesses were about to close.

"Enough, Mimi!", Kristina nearly shouted, unable to contain herself. "You're a spoiled brat—my feet hurt; I can't walk. Go, try to find me some kind of footwear, disappear for a bit—I can't take you anymore, I'm not budging."

And, turning her back bluntly, she started to rub her aching legs.

Mimi cast her a look of hatred and walked away with stiff, childlike steps. Still annoyed, Kristina ordered a coffee and decided to stare at the sea until her anger passed. That's what she got for drifting around. Behind her, the woman from that morning was gathering her things and singing a strange song; the fabrics, outspread, resembled shrouds. Kristina thought that there, in the vague horizon, she could make out the gleaming edges of Corfu, and she dreamed of being in Mr. Tassi's mansion. Yes, that night she would go to bed with him. The girl would soon appear with some form of comfortable footwear; it had been a very long day and she had lost her temper, but she was calming down now. With its speedy wake, the patrol boat broke the water's surface. A voice broke her out of her trance:

"Looks like friend not coming. Not coming."

"She'll be here, we have to go back on the next ferry. What about your sons?"

"Not sons, one is nephew, other is future son-in-law. They practice music, my daughter is getting married."

The woman had a surprisingly gentle voice; turning around, Kristina smiled at her:

"You must be happy, is she the oldest?"

"Not oldest, youngest, many grandchildren now. Many children, many grandchildren, lots of work paying for wedding. I selling here, then Italy. Albanians poor."

"Ah, I'm also going back to Italy." And Kristina pictured the orange purse she missed so dearly, which must still be resting in the hotel closet. She felt that the wedding's good tidings included her in some way:

"You see, I'm waiting for my friend to get the ferry—I didn't bring anything, not even to pay for this coffee. . ."

They were putting away the chairs in the bar, and the waiter approached Kristina with the check.

"The ferry?" The woman folded the last tablecloth and stood there staring at her and humming.

Kristina smiled at her; if she had the chance she would return to Saranda and buy those embroideries; she thought of giving the woman a few coins, then she remembered that she didn't have a cent on her: she would ask Mimi. She thought she heard a high-pitched voice calling her from behind and turned around smiling, but it was just a boy running off.

"The ferry? The ferry?" The woman had gathered all of her merchandise by now. "Ah, poor thing, your foot bad, bad gold sandals. You poor little thing, poor thing. You lost, I think, you want hotel?"—and the woman, as if she had known Kristina her whole life, sat by her side and started stroking her as she said, as if in a soft lament: "Ferry cannot be today, it left fifteen minutes ago. Tomorrow, tomorrow."

She remembers the previous evening as a living nightmare; she remembers how she cried in the arms of a woman who, suddenly, had approached her; she remembers how she threw herself into those unknown arms until she could feel their warmth. Shameful. The woman, as if it were her duty in life, had started rocking her, saying "poor thing" over and over again. Kristina had sunk into her warm and fragrant breast—at the first "poor thing" she felt miserable, at the second, tremendously childish, at the third defenseless, and as the Albanian woman cradled her repeating "poor thing," she wished to come undone, to die—all of her life's mistakes came to mind: the train in Angoulême that meaningless morning, the face of the boy who now seemed to be, oddly enough, the only lost opportunity in this absurd journey.

Drowning in pity, stammering, she tried to tell everything to that warm chest, yet not only did the Albanian woman not seem to care much about her story, but she had also started singing softly and was stroking her hair, cradling her like her own daughter; "there, there," she said, drying Kristina's tears with the edge of her blouse. That's what made her break down. How long had it been since anyone treated her like this? How long since anyone consoled her? How long since a body approached her without asking for anything in return? When she managed to pull herself together, she realized that she could barely walk; limping she let herself be dragged by the woman and her nephew, who had come out of nowhere; they carried her home almost flying, made her leave her sandals outside, and, finally, laid her down on the divan.

"You, Poor Thing, here, relax," the woman said. And then she disappeared.

She slept as though she were falling into a well and woke up lost, letting her gaze wander over the rugs that covered everything, the fleuron upholstery, the ornate ceramics. The sound of dishes and aroma of olive oil reached her. All of a sudden, Mirvei entered and looked at her, beaming.

"Better? Sleep well? Come on, you eat with us."

And then she touched her ample bosom:

"I'm Mirvei."

"And I'm Kristina."

"Yes, you. You, Poor Thing."

In the house lived various families, whose groupings Kristina was unable to distinguish; half-dressed children who peeked out and stared at her indiscreetly, sticky little hands that approached to touch her hair, smiling adults who didn't seem to pay her much attention. In the center of the table there was rice, an oily soup, sausages. She would have killed for a coffee, but she convinced herself that, at the end of the day, this wasn't so different from an English breakfast. As she filled her plate, Mirvei repeated, "I'm Mirvei," touching her heart, as if it were crucial for Kristina to remember her name. Slightly bewildered, she also touched her heart and alternated between repeating "Mirvei" or "Kristina"; that seemed to make the woman happy and also some of the children, who pointed at her and burst into laughter. Her ankle was hurting less. Mirvei was now wiping the snot off a child who was kicking up a fuss and who was probably one of her grandchildren, although he could also have been one of her children. Every once in a while she would say, "eat, eat," and then, "Bless those eyes of yours," covering him in kisses. As the boy squirmed with pleasure, she kept an eye on Kristina, who was timidly holding out her plate; then she would go back to making sure she was eating, pointing at her—"Poor Thing, Poor Thing"—as if that were the only explanation the family needed for her to sit at their table. In one corner there was a very old, old woman, with large gold earrings. She stared at Kristina with little marble eyes but didn't say anything. As quickly as the dishes had been set, the table was cleared and everyone vanished, leaving the two alone in the living room. At first Kristina wandered around studying the objects. Then she sat in front of the old woman and kept silent. The woman started rocking back and forth like a wind-up doll, then she whimpered, repeating a single sentence that Kristina was unable to understand, but she was so exhausted that she decided to immerse herself in the lament like a mantra. An hour later Mirvei reappeared, looking like she had cleaned the entire house. She sat by her side, dried the old woman's tears, blew her nose and held her in her arms, like a little idol.

"Why is she crying?"

"The loss of Kosovo, every day a bit."

"And what's she saying?"

"I don't know, very old language. There are a lot of these old people, lots of these tears, one in every family. But we're not going to Kosovo, tomorrow Italy. That's how it has to be: everyone has their own trade. Good? I don't have money, Poor Thing, but boat easy. Albanians cross all the time, tablecloths on train to Ancona, good for tourists, they say Italian embroidery, but my mother-in-law makes them."

And Mirvei let out a clean laugh.

"But careful for patrol. Look, wedding dress," and she showed her a black material that the old woman had been embroidering at some point.

Then she unfolded something that looked like a house-coat with large antique fleurons and told her:

"Tomorrow you dress Albanian, better." Then, very amused, she pulled some shoes out of the bag, taking Kristina by the hands: "And shoes. Free your feet, free your life. Poor Thing"—she insisted as she pet her—"Your hair beautiful, very red, so beautiful. But you know what? Better scarf, so no one sees it."

It's still night when she feels a hand shaking her; jumping out of her sleep she sees that, dressed in all black, her head wrapped in a scarf, Mirvei is whispering:

"Don't be scared, Poor Thing, not scared. A little quiet, yes. And Albanian clothes. Help me with bags. Scarf, scarf."

She gets dressed stumbling, barely has time to realize what is happening when Mirvei loads her with embroidered tablecloths. She will come back to Albania. She will come back to see Mirvei and pay her for everything she's been doing like it's the most natural thing in the world. Yes, she will come back to Albania, but right now the only thing that matters is reaching Sirolo, the soothing pots of hydrangeas; she'll get her orange handbag back; she never dreamed that her honeymoon would end like this, disguised and on a boat with a clandestine group of migrants. Almost there, she thinks, almost there. Mirvei, increasingly nervous, rambles on:

"I go to Ancona, Poor Thing, work for a while as cleaner, or whatever, if tablecloths don't work out in Ancona I go to Milan. Don't be lazy, you, new shoes. Run, boat is there."

The fresh end-of-night air hits her as she follows the group of Albanians; she sees the leader of the expedition going up to Mirvei and telling her off. Simian features, hard jaw, greedy, brutal eyes. She doesn't understand what they are saying, but it doesn't look good—everything seems to point to the leader not wanting her to get on the boat. Without thinking it over too much, Mirvei takes a handful of bills out of her pocket and hands them to the man.

"Boss is scared, the red hair. I give money, you repay me sometime. Let's go, Poor Thing, very bad temper, have to obey."

And she smiles almost, as if saying sorry.

Before getting on the boat, Kristina looks back and sees the house with its clay tiles; she thinks of the elderly woman with gold earrings and imagines being pierced by her little eyes, judged for taking money away from Mirvei. How hard it all is, how sad. Minutes after they leave the coast, Mirvei, with startling strength and brusqueness, puts her hand on Kristina's head, forcing her to hide.

Reaching Ancona is the only thought that gets Kristina through the journey—reaching Ancona is her amulet, her talisman—she repeats it like a prayer: reaching Ancona, and the creaking wood, the smell, the dangerous sea. So as not to be spotted, she has to stay hidden among the feet of the presumed fishermen every time the Italian speedboat polices the sea and the men's legs tense with nerves. The journey won't take long, Mirvei has told her, one shore is very close to the other; everything is the same on this side of the world, a lick of water, a shot of foam—here there have never been borders, just police. A car will be waiting to bring them to the train; they'll have to be careful, very careful so that no one asks for their papers.

"Yes," Kristina says, shaking her head because she has to stay silent: reaching Ancona.

From Ancona to Sirolo it's not too far; this time she'll have to make the journey on foot. And she remembers the taxi driver who brought her to the hotel, Mr. Tassi's yacht, the creature comforts that now feel like part of another life. Reaching Ancona. She crosses her fingers.

"Everything is going to change."

Mirvei puts her finger over her lips, her face shining with sweat; fear peers out of her eyes, but she hasn't lost her smile, that thin-lipped smile. Kristina must have spoken out loud, because the boss is berating Mirvei again, gripping her arm with his claw-like fingers; he's a crude man, his dirty boots close to Mirvei's face, so close. He studies Kristina with lust—sometimes he looks at her like he's about to tear off her clothes, sometimes he treats her like something to be sold or thrown off deck. Out of vengeance he devotes himself to bothering Mirvei, grabbing her hair, pinching her arm, pretending he's going to burn her with his cigarette. But Mirvei is clever; she acts submissive, and later, when the boss isn't looking, she slyly rolls her eyes to show Kristina to be patient—this man's a fool—she seems to say; he's crazy, don't pay him any attention.

The sun rises and heats the boat, stabbing needles into the women's backs, drawing out the strong smells of sea and men. If she could peek out, she would see the coast, but the men don't let her. A speedboat's motor hums. What would happen if they caught her, if they found her hidden among Albanians? Mirvei takes her hand, brings it to her heart, and puts another finger over her lips, which are now moving as if in prayer.

They arrive with no more scares than the speedboat guarding the border; stretching their arms and legs, they clean themselves up to look less suspicious, Mirvei says, less suspicious. In the car Mirvei adjusts her scarf, takes her by the arm. On land, Kristina thinks, there's more danger. If they're caught at sea they'll just be sent home, but what happens if they're found in Italy? The olive trees overlap with the first traces of the city, plastic bags float in the air, industrial warehouses emerge.

It's past noon when they reach the station; Mirvei offers her a piece of cheese and adjusts her scarf again. Kristina would like to thank her for everything, but Mirvei seems too nervous to listen, and she sits her down where no one can see her; there's still some time before the train leaves. She seems very anxious about looking after the bag with her tablecloths; she checks the luggage, looks for something in her handbag. They'll catch a regional train; soon they'll be in Ancona.

"In Ancona," Mirvei repeats, "and there, free like the wind, Poor Thing. You free, I do my things."

Kristina focuses on the image of her orange handbag, the money and documents, the clothes stored in the closet. Putting on boots again, what a luxury. Yes, soon this nightmare, this torment will end; she tries not to think, feeling the touch of Mirvei's arm—it's so warm that she feels a rush of tenderness. They only have a while left, just an hour before she's Kristina again, not Cleavage, not Poor Thing. The sky, crystal clear, announces the end of summer. She dozes off, and when she wakes, Mirvei is tugging at her, whispering that the train is about to enter the station. She gets up pushing the bundles, so nervous she can't sit down; she leans out the window and the air hits her in the face; two red locks escape from her scarf. Mirvei gives her a stern look, covers her again, hides her, takes her by the arm as if afraid someone will tear her away; despite her age she makes energetic movements, just her presence calms Kristina, but the anguish returns; for a moment she fades into this deformed and twisted life that doesn't belong to her, losing herself in a concave mirror where she is not herself but rather someone born in another country, another world—where she is not Kristina, not even Cleavage, but a migrant, a nameless Albanian woman, much more Poor Thing than anything else.

A whistle announces their departure; she's about to sit down when she sees a silver train stop right in front of her window. The passengers, sitting on comfortable seats, are reading newspapers, dozing off. Nostalgic, she tells herself that tomorrow, surely, she'll be traveling on something just as expensive; she'll go back to being one of those beings who is indifferent to luxury, foreign to the pitiful humiliation of comparisons. How sweet the lives of others, how easy, and suddenly she sees, among the confusion of faces, one that looks familiar. It's like a dream, but little by little the vague contour comes into focus and she recognizes, yes, she recognizes that dark-haired boy she saw centuries ago— on another train, in another life, in another world—among the distracted passengers his profile emerges: the boy from Angoulême. Kristina watches him in shock; his hair is longer, and he's holding a guidebook in his hands. At first she doesn't react, then she shyly waves at him, then more forcefully; she wants to speak to him; she beats the window with her fists, shaking her arms. By the time the train starts moving she's about to shout, but she senses the danger; containing herself she calms down, closes her eyes and lets Mirvei hold her.

Suddenly, the young man looks up from his reading and out the window. Across the track there's an old train, and through its dirty windows he discerns two women who are wearing clothes from another time. They must be mother and daughter; the older one is embracing and scolding the younger one, who has her eyes closed. Next to him a student, possibly American, points at them with one finger:

"Albanians," he says, "be careful. They get on trains and rob people."

Then:

"What's your name?"

The young man is happy to have a new travel companion; he's a freckled blond, studying business or something like that; it's nice to chat with different people, get to know other perspectives. By the way, where is Albania? He glances at his guidebook and closes it; they're about to leave the station— it's the thrill of travel, the desire for adventure, the promise of the red-haired woman who fettered him in Angoulême.

The trains are already moving; they cross and separate, and for one second they remain side by side. Framed by the shadows in the train car, he makes out the two Albanian women, who, in the cottony twilight, appear painted. Then the scene breaks; they're picking up speed while the other train enters into its rattle of the past. Impulsively, the young man presses himself against the glass and looks back towards the pale blue that blurs the image. And that's when he sees, waving in the wind, the slight hand of a woman who is leaving.

The Miraculous Spiral

Eadem mutata resurgo.[1]
—Jakob Bernoulli

Napoleon: They tell me you have written this large book on the system of the universe without ever mentioning its Creator.
Laplace: Sir, I had no need of that hypothesis.
Conversation about the book *Exposition du système du monde,*
by Pierre-Simon Laplace

AS THE heads are falling, the woman loses herself in the mathematics books that pile up in her husband's library. She's not allowed, but due to the riots they've closed the monastery where she used to study, so now she does it in secret and takes chickpeas from the kitchen to use as an abacus. If they hadn't forced her to marry an old man, she would spend all her time deciphering mathematical operations. Now she drugs herself with the infinite pleasure of calculations. Around her every-

---

1 Although changed, I rise again the same.

thing is death, even in peaceful Normandy, so she's decided not to pay attention to what surrounds her.

When she's able to escape her husband's watchful gaze, she goes for walks on the beach. On one of those walks she found a conch, its pinkish shell full of holes; since then she collects them, hiding them in her chamber—using a sharpened rock she wears down one, two, three, a hundred, discovering that they all swirl identically. She does calculations and sketches the spiral. It's not constant, like the one Archimedes postulated—dull and foreseeable—but one containing a tiny cosmos that opens up like a whirlwind, in geometric progression, spinning in a curve that grows wider and wider. The rotation is familiar to her: she's seen it on her son's navel, on spiders' patient webs, in soup starting to swirl in its pot, on sunflower heads, pregnant with seeds. She's also pregnant and in her last month. She waddles towards the beach, between the grazing cattle and the apple orchards. If her husband finds out that she's escaped again, he'll lock her in the bedroom. She hates him, and she also hates her destiny. She doesn't want the burden of this child, just as she never wished for the first one, who still doesn't even know how to walk, nor will she want or love those who arrive in the coming years. She's terrified of that struggle against death that is childbirth, her red blood staining everything. She's not yet sixteen, and her only wish is to lock herself in the library and calculate the rotation of that constant spiral in its radius, or maybe take off the bonnet that's holding her head prisoner, or throw her shawl to the wind and let it gallop like a horse. But she covers her shoulders: if she gets sick, then she would really be lost. At least now, while the wet nurse takes care of the little one, she's free to think about whatever she wants. Holding her belly, she starts to walk down to the beach. Her muslin dress sticks to her, dampened and waving in the sea breeze. Tired, she sits on the rocks and sees something shining amid the tight green field: it's a minted coin from who knows where, engraved with a woman dressed almost like her and a phrase: *In God we trust*. Somewhat blurry, an impossible date reads: 1944. It must be one of those rare pieces with erroneous information. Or maybe it's fake; it has a curious hole, as if pierced by a pellet. The finding makes her happy—it must be a talisman, so she hangs it on the fine chain she wears around her neck and, now calmer, continues her descent. Polyhedrons, cylinders, cones, spheres. The sphere and the spiral that emerges inside the shell, its mysterious growing orbit. Does it repeat in the universe? Reaching the shore, she wets one shoe in the water—she likes to see how the trim dampens—and the silk pompom comes off the toe, sinking into the sea. How long before it turns into sand? No one knows where things end. And she, how will she meet her end? Is now her time to die, or will she end up bursting in her tenth delivery? How long does it take our consciousness to leave us?

How long for a severed head to lose its memories? She imagines them taking her to the gallows like they did to Charlotte, the blonde girl she studied with at the monastery in Caen. Her childhood was left behind in Caen, along with her parents' home, since she was forced to follow a husband to the rustic expanses of Pointe du Hoc. "A wealthy husband, with land." And her mother, lowering her voice in a gluttonous tone: "One of the *old* families." Charlotte was a little older and led her by the hand to the study hall, defended her from the older students' tricks and from the tedium of the little ones. She used to help her with numbers and schoolwork. She would read her stories when she couldn't sleep. Her long, blonde braid and the scent of her hair, no doubt clipped by the executioner, her cheeks so close, so close. Now she imagines her severed head; she imagines the head watching her with bulging eyes, muttering "run, run"; she imagines the blood that falls, flooding everything, engulfing the gallows, the street, the study hall and the refectory, the chapel and its chalice, the white cups from breakfast. Waves of blood that are also hers, the young woman says to herself, they will both meet bloody ends, only hers will come without theatrics, devoid of any paraphernalia, anonymous: no one remembers a woman who dies in childbirth.

It's a morning with violent clouds; the waves have withdrawn, crashing against the rocks and revealing the sand's nakedness. The sea, pinkish in the sunrise, is now the color of cloudy wine. With a stick, the girl starts to draw in the sand, as if it were one giant parchment: one curve, then another, and another, each one wider than the last, circles that become infinite, again and again until she's exhausted, can barely breathe; the whole beach is a map of this eternal rotation that mirrors the sky. Struggling, she climbs the cliff and contemplates her work. The solution to her problem is there. If she were to follow the spiral in the opposite direction, she thinks, if she were to search for its origin by walking from the outside to the center, she would have to turn in infinite circles. But if she only considers the path formed by that string of sand, it would be as measurable as the coarsest rope sold by a peddler. But can something be measurable and infinite at the same time? Such a wonder can only be defined in a dead language. "*Spira mirabilis*," the girl shouts in Latin, "*Spira mirabilis!*" Her voice comes and goes, striking against the rocks. It's so beautiful that she feels dizzy.

The wall of cliffs cuts into the sand and reflects a dying sun; a hawk circles its prey. Soon, when shadows arrive in this endless space, mysterious galaxies will extend the spiral of their arms.

The girl feels a sudden pain in her stomach; something contracts and then relaxes again. Anxious, she keeps climbing, but the pain is sharp: the cramps are coming faster and faster, faster. On the verge of fainting, she realizes that the most prudent thing to do would be to return home, but the idea fills her with horror. What if she fled? No, she doesn't have a way out, maybe she and her child should walk towards the violet surface and drown themselves. She falls flat on the naked earth. As if understanding, from somewhere in the species, what is about to occur, a cow trots up to her. She lowers her nape, snorting, and licks the girl's arm, perhaps attracted to the salty aftertaste. The girl cries out, writhing, pushing down on her belly—if only she could empty it like a wineskin but she can't breathe, she feels like she's about to die; squatting she sheds a viscous fluid, at last a shock of sudden blood rushes between her legs, she closes her eyes because a black sea is sucking the life out of her, the child is not coming out, she roars in pain, cursing, with a final and bestial drive she spits out the son that stamped her entrails. Exhausted, she places him on her breast: then she doesn't think anything, doesn't feel anything. Everything goes dark.

The moon, immense, rises behind the hill, illuminating the two bodies in a reverberation of still flesh. The noises of the night have not yet begun, and nothing moves in the milky silence. The bloodstain forms a halo on the muslin dress, her bonnet has fallen off and the silk bow is knotted at her throat. Soon a wail can be heard, and a trembling little body squirms on top of its mother, roots in the air, shakes, moves its arms, fills its lungs; bursting with life it starts to howl.

The torches of the search party have passed through their shelter of flowerbeds and cupolas, the hedge maze, the waving cypresses; the gravel paths crunch and fill with shouts that penetrate the countryside, repeating the woman's name. The wet nurse finds them. She lowers her flame to the unfortunate woman's face, closes her eyes and, foreseeing the men's gazes, lowers her skirts. Then she picks up the trembling mass, wrapping it in her shawl. And before they can find a stretcher to move the deceased woman, she's already cooing at the little one next to the hearth.

Below, on the beach, outlined in the sand, the spiral turns again and again, extending in growing curves, replicating itself in swirls, infinite rings of inexplicable beauty. In a little while, with the high tide, the drawing and its mystery will have been washed away.

THANK YOU to Pedro Alejandre, Armando Minguzzi, Bárbara Pierpaoli and María Roces for their travel stories. Thank you to José Carrasco, for the gift of an image. To Corina Gorbato, for certain family memories. To Marta Espinós, for her contagious passion for conch shells. To Martín Obligado and Natalia Ares, for explaining some principles of physics. To Montse Armengou and Ricard Belis, for their book *Convoy 927*, on which part of "Silence" is based. To María Luisa Ramos, for the painful retelling of her journey to Mauthausen and for the hospitality at her home in Asturias. To Raquel Gisbert, Carola Aikin and Nuria Sierra, to my sister María and my daughter Camila, for their critical and insightful readings. To those around me, as always, for their infinite tolerance.

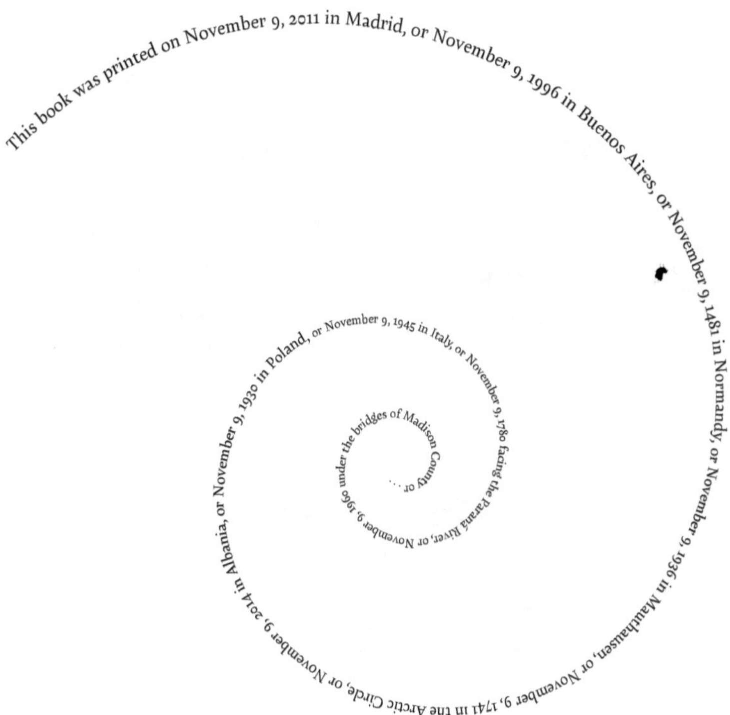

This book was printed on November 9, 2011 in Madrid, or November 9, 1996 in Buenos Aires, or November 9, 1481 in Normandy, or November 9, 1936 in Mauthausen, or November 9, 1741 in the Arctic Circle, or November 9, 2014 in Albania, or November 9, 1930 in Poland, or November 9, 1945 in Italy, or November 9, 1780 facing the Paraná River, or November 9, 1960 under the bridges of Madison County, or . . .

CLARA OBLIGADO was born in Buenos Aires. A political exile, she has lived in Spain since 1976. She has been awarded the Lumen women's prize and the Juan March Cencillo short novel prize, along with the Setenil award for *El libro de los viajes equivocados* in 2012. Some of her short story collections are *Las otras vidas, El libro de los viajes equivocados, La muerte juega a los dados*, and *La biblioteca de agua* and among her essay collections are *Una casa lejos de casa. La escritura extranjera* and *Todo lo que crece. Naturaleza y escritura.*

MOLLY WAGSCHAL is a recipient of the 2023 Sundial House Literary Translation Award. She translates from Spanish and Catalan into English and is pursuing a Ph.D. in Hispanic Studies at Brown University.

GPSR Authorized Representative: Easy Access System Europe, Mustamäe tee
50, 10621 Tallinn, Estonia, gpsr.requests@easproject.com